TRUMAN CAPOTE

The Grass Harp

Truman Capote was a native of New Orleans, where he was born on September 30, 1924. His first novel, *Other Voices, Other Rooms,* was an international literary success when first published in 1948, and accorded the author a prominent place among the writers of America's postwar generation. He sustained this position subsequently with short-story collections (*A Tree of Night,* among others), novels and novellas (*The Grass Harp* and *Breakfast at Tiffany's*), some of the best travel writing of our time (*Local Color*), profiles and reportage that appeared originally in *The New Yorker* (*The Duke in His Domain* and *The Muses Are Heard*), a true-crime masterpiece (*In Cold Blood*), several short memoirs about his childhood in the South (*A Christmas Memory, The Thanksgiving Visitor*, and *One Christmas*), two plays (*The Grass Harp* and *House of Flowers*), and two films (*Beat the Devil* and *The Innocents*).

Mr. Capote twice won the O. Henry Memorial Short Story Prize and was a member of the National Institute of Arts and Letters. He died in August 1984, shortly before his sixtieth birthday.

INTERNATIONAL

Also by TRUMAN CAPOTE

The Grass Harp

TRUMAN CAPOTE

The Grass Harp

VINTAGE INTERNATIONAL

VINTAGE BOOKS

A DIVISION OF RANDOM HOUSE, INC.

NEW YORK

FIRST VINTAGE INTERNATIONAL EDITION, NOVEMBER 1995

Copyright © 1951 by Truman Capote
Copyright renewed 1979 by Truman Capote

Library of Congress Cataloging-in-Publication Data
Capote, Truman, 1924–1984
The grass harp / Truman Capote. — 1st Vintage International ed.
p. cm.
ISBN 0-679-76670-7
I. Title.
PS3505.A59G7 1993
813'.54—dc20 93-19633
CIP

Manufactured in the United States of America
10 9 8 7 6 5 4 3

for Miss Sook Faulk
In memory of affections deep and true

The Grass Harp

One

WHEN was it that first I heard of the grass harp? Long before the autumn we lived in the China tree; an earlier autumn, then; and of course it was Dolly who told me, no one else would have known to call it that, a grass harp.

If on leaving town you take the church road you soon will pass a glaring hill of bonewhite slabs and brown burnt flowers: this is the Baptist cemetery. Our people, Talbos, Fenwicks, are buried there; my mother lies next to my father, and the graves of kinfolk, twenty or more, are around them like the prone roots of a stony tree. Below the hill grows a field of high Indian grass that changes color with the seasons: go to see it in the fall, late September, when it has gone red as sunset, when scarlet shadows like firelight breeze over it and the autumn winds strum on its dry leaves sighing human music, a harp of voices.

Beyond the field begins the darkness of River Woods. It must have been on one of those September days when we were there in the woods gathering roots that Dolly said: Do you hear? that is the grass harp, always telling a story—it knows the stories of all the people on the hill, of all the people who ever lived, and when we are dead it will tell ours, too.

After my mother died, my father, a traveling man, sent me to live with his cousins, Verena and Dolly Talbo, two unmarried ladies who were sisters. Before that, I'd not ever been allowed into their house. For reasons no one ever got quite clear, Verena and my father did not speak. Probably Papa asked Verena to lend him some money, and she refused; or perhaps she did make the loan, and he never returned it. You can be sure that the trouble was over money, because nothing else would have mattered to them so much, especially Verena, who was the richest person in town. The drugstore, the drygoods store, a filling station, a grocery, an office building, all this was hers, and the earning of it had not made her an easy woman.

Anyway, Papa said he would never set foot inside her house. He told such terrible things about the Talbo ladies. One of the stories he spread, that Verena was a morphodyte, has never stopped going around, and the ridicule he heaped on Miss Dolly Talbo was too much even for my mother: she told him he ought to be ashamed, mocking anyone so gentle and harmless.

I think they were very much in love, my mother and father. She used to cry every time he went away to sell his frigidaires. He married her when she was sixteen; she did not live to be thirty. The afternoon she died Papa, calling her name, tore off all his clothes and ran out naked into the yard.

It was the day after the funeral that Verena came to the house. I remember the terror of watching her move up the walk, a whip-thin, handsome woman with shingled peppersalt hair, black, rather virile eyebrows and a dainty cheekmole. She opened the front door and walked right into the house. Since the funeral, Papa had been breaking things, not with fury, but quietly, thoroughly: he would amble into the parlor, pick up a china figure, muse over it a moment, then throw it against the wall. The floor and stairs were littered with cracked glass, scattered silverware; a ripped nightgown, one of my mother's, hung over the banister.

Verena's eyes flicked over the debris. "Eugene, I want a word with you," she said in that hearty, coldly exalted voice, and Papa answered: "Yes, sit down, Verena. I thought you would come."

That afternoon Dolly's friend Catherine Creek came over and packed my clothes, and Papa drove me to the impressive, shadowy house on Talbo Lane. As I was getting out of the car he tried to hug me, but I was scared of him and wriggled out of his arms. I'm sorry now that we did not hug each other. Because a few days later, on his way up to Mobile, his car skidded and fell fifty feet into the Gulf. When I saw him again there were silver dollars weighting down his eyes.

Except to remark that I was small for my age, a runt, no one had ever paid any attention to me; but now people pointed me out, and said wasn't it sad? that poor little Collin Fenwick! I tried to look pitiful because I knew it pleased people: every man in town must have treated me to a Dixie Cup or a box of Crackerjack, and at school I got good grades for the first time. So it was a long while before I calmed down enough to notice Dolly Talbo.

And when I did I fell in love.

Imagine what it must have been for her when first I came to the house, a loud and prying boy of eleven. She skittered at the sound of my footsteps or, if there was no avoiding me, folded like the petals of shy-lady fern. She was one of those people who can disguise themselves as an object in the room, a shadow in the corner, whose presence is a delicate happening. She wore the quietest shoes, plain virginal dresses with hems that touched her ankles. Though older than her sister, she seemed someone who, like myself, Verena had adopted. Pulled and guided by the gravity of Verena's planet, we rotated separately in the outer spaces of the house.

In the attic, a slipshod museum spookily peopled with old display dummies from Verena's drygoods store, there were many loose boards, and by inching these I could look down into almost any room. Dolly's room, unlike the rest of the house, which bulged with fat dour furniture, contained only a bed, a bureau, a chair: a nun might have lived there, except for one fact: the walls, everything was painted an outlandish pink, even the floor was this color. Whenever I spied on Dolly, she usually was to be seen doing one of two things: she was standing in front of a mirror snipping with a pair of garden shears her yellow and white, already brief hair; either that, or she was writing in pencil on a pad of coarse Kress paper. She kept wetting the pencil on the tip of her tongue, and sometimes she spoke aloud a sentence as she put it down: *Do not touch sweet foods like candy and salt will kill you for certain.* Now I'll tell you, she was writing letters. But at first this correspondence was a puzzle to me. After all, her only friend was Catherine Creek, she saw no one else and she never left the house, except once a week when she and Catherine went to River Woods where they gathered the ingredients of a dropsy remedy Dolly brewed and bottled. Later I discovered she had customers for

this medicine throughout the state, and it was to them that her
many letters were addressed.

Verena's room, connecting with Dolly's by a passage, was
rigged up like an office. There was a rolltop desk, a library of
ledgers, filing cabinets. After supper, wearing a green eyeshade,
she would sit at her desk totaling figures and turning the pages
of her ledgers until even the street-lamps had gone out. Though
on diplomatic, political terms with many people, Verena had
no close friends at all. Men were afraid of her, and she herself
seemed to be afraid of women. Some years before she had
been greatly attached to a blonde jolly girl called Maudie Laura
Murphy, who worked for a bit in the post office here and who
finally married a liquor salesman from St. Louis. Verena had
been very bitter over this and said publicly that the man was
no account. It was therefore a surprise when, as a wedding
present, she gave the couple a honeymoon trip to the Grand
Canyon. Maudie and her husband never came back; they
opened a filling station nearby Grand Canyon, and from time
to time sent Verena Kodak snapshots of themselves. These
pictures were a pleasure and a grief. There were nights when
she never opened her ledgers, but sat with her forehead leaning
in her hands, and the pictures spread on the desk. After she
had put them away, she would pace around the room with
the lights turned off, and presently there would come a hurt
rusty crying sound as though she'd tripped and fallen in the
dark.

That part of the attic from which I could have looked down
into the kitchen was fortified against me, for it was stacked
with trunks like bales of cotton. At that time it was the kitchen
I most wanted to spy upon; this was the real living room of the
house, and Dolly spent most of the day there chatting with her
friend Catherine Creek. As a child, an orphan, Catherine
Creek had been hired out to Mr. Uriah Talbo, and they had all
grown up together, she and the Talbo sisters, there on the old
farm that has since become a railroad depot. Dolly she called
Dollyheart, but Verena she called That One. She lived in the
back yard in a tin-roofed silvery little house set among sunflowers and trellises of butterbean vine. She claimed to be an
Indian, which made most people wink, for she was dark as the
angels of Africa. But for all I know it may have been true:
certainly she dressed like an Indian. That is, she had a string
of turquoise beads, and wore enough rouge to put out your
eyes; it shone on her cheeks like votive taillights. Most of her
teeth were gone; she kept her jaws jacked up with cotton wad-

ding, and Verena would say Dammit Catherine, since you can't make a sensible sound why in creation won't you go down to Doc Crocker and let him put some teeth in your head? It was true that she was hard to understand: Dolly was the only one who could fluently translate her friend's muffled, mumbling noises. It was enough for Catherine that Dolly understood her: they were always together and everything they had to say they said to each other: bending my ear to an attic beam I could hear the tantalizing tremor of their voices flowing like sapsyrup through the old wood.

To reach the attic, you climbed a ladder in the linen closet, the ceiling of which was a trapdoor. One day, as I started up, I saw that the trapdoor was swung open and, listening, heard above me an idle sweet humming, like the pretty sounds small girls make when they are playing alone. I would have turned back, but the humming stopped, and a voice said: "Catherine?"

"Collin," I answered, showing myself.

The snowflake of Dolly's face held its shape; for once she did not dissolve. "This is where you come—we wondered," she said, her voice frail and crinkling as tissue paper. She had the eyes of a gifted person, kindled, transparent eyes, luminously green as mint jelly: gazing at me through the attic twilight they admitted, timidly, that I meant her no harm. "You play games up here—in the attic? I told Verena you would be lonesome." Stooping, she rooted around in the depths of a barrel. "Here now," she said, "you can help me by looking in that other barrel. I'm hunting for a coral castle; and a sack of pearl pebbles, all colors. I think Catherine will like that, a bowl of goldfish, don't you? For her birthday. We used to have a bowl of tropical fish—devils, they were: ate each other up. But I remember when we bought them; we went all the way to Brewton, sixty miles. I never went sixty miles before, and I don't know that I ever will again. Ah see, here it is, the castle." Soon afterwards I found the pebbles; they were like kernels of corn or candy, and: "Have a piece of candy," I said, offering the sack. "Oh thank you," she said, "I love a piece of candy, even when it tastes like a pebble."

We were friends, Dolly and Catherine and me. I was eleven, then I was sixteen. Though no honors came my way, those were the lovely years.

I never brought anyone home with me, and I never wanted to. Once I took a girl to the picture show, and on the way home she asked couldn't she come in for a drink of water. If

I'd thought she was really thirsty I would've said all right; but I knew she was faking just so she could see inside the house the way people were always wanting to, and so I told her she better wait until she got home. She said: "All the world knows Dolly Talbo's gone, and you're gone too." I liked that girl well enough, but I gave her a shove anyway, and she said her brother would fix my wagon, which he did: right here at the corner of my mouth I've still got a scar where he hit me with a Coca-Cola bottle.

I know: Dolly, they said, was Verena's cross, and said, too, that more went on in the house on Talbo Lane than a body cared to think about. Maybe so. But those were the lovely years.

On winter afternoons, as soon as I came in from school, Catherine hustled open a jar of preserves, while Dolly put a foot-high pot of coffee on the stove and pushed a pan of biscuits into the oven; and the oven, opening, would let out a hot vanilla fragrance, for Dolly, who lived off sweet foods, was always baking a pound cake, raisin bread, some kind of cookie or fudge: never would touch a vegetable, and the only meat she liked was the chicken brain, a pea-sized thing gone before you've tasted it. What with a woodstove and an open fireplace, the kitchen was warm as a cow's tongue. The nearest winter came was to frost the windows with its zero blue breath. If some wizard would like to make me a present, let him give me a bottle filled with the voices of that kitchen, the ha ha ha and fire whispering, a bottle brimming with its buttery sugary bakery smells—though Catherine smelled like a sow in the spring. It looked more like a cozy parlor than a kitchen; there was a hook rug on the floor, rocking chairs; ranged along the walls were pictures of kittens, an enthusiasm of Dolly's; there was a geranium plant that bloomed, then bloomed again all year round, and Catherine's goldfish, in a bowl on the oilcloth-covered table, fanned their tails through the portals of the coral castle. Sometimes we worked jigsaw puzzles, dividing the pieces among us, and Catherine would hide pieces if she thought you were going to finish your part of the puzzle before she finished hers. Or they would help with my homework; that was a mess. About all natural things Dolly was sophisticated; she had the subterranean intelligence of a bee that knows where to find the sweetest flower: she could tell you of a storm a day in advance, predict the fruit of the fig tree, lead you to mushrooms and wild honey, a hidden nest of guinea hen eggs. She looked around her, and felt what she saw. But about homework Dolly was as ignorant as Catherine. "America must have been called America before Columbus came. It stands to reason. Otherwise, how would he have known it was America?" And Catherine said: "That's correct. America is an old Indian word." Of the two, Catherine was the worst: she insisted on her infallibility, and if you did not write down exactly what she said, she got jumpy and spilled the coffee or something. But I never listened to her again after what she said about Lincoln: that he was part Negro and part Indian and only a speck white. Even I knew this was not true. But I am under special obligation to Catherine; if it had not been for her who knows whether I would have grown to ordinary human size? At fourteen I was not much bigger than Biddy Skinner, and people told how he'd had offers from a circus. Catherine said don't worry yourself honey, all you need is a little stretching. She pulled at my arms, legs, tugged at my head as though it were an apple latched to an unyielding bough. But it's the truth that within two years she'd stretched me from four feet nine to five feet seven, and I can prove it by the breadknife knotches on the pantry door, for even now when so much has gone, when there is only wind in the stove and winter in the kitchen, those growing-up scars are still there, a testimony.

Despite the generally beneficial effect Dolly's medicine appeared to have on those who sent for it, letters once in a while came saying Dear Miss Talbo we won't be needing any more dropsy cure on account of poor Cousin Belle (or whoever) passed away last week bless her soul. Then the kitchen was a mournful place; with folded hands and nodding heads my two friends bleakly recalled the circumstances of the case, and Well, Catherine would say, we did the best we could Dollyheart, but the good Lord had other notions. Verena, too, could make the kitchen sad, as she was always introducing a new rule or enforcing an old one: do, don't, stop, start: it was as though we were clocks she kept an eye on to see that our time jibed with her own, and woe if we were ten minutes fast, an hour slow: Verena went off like a cuckoo. That One! said Catherine, and Dolly would go hush now! hush now! as though to quiet not Catherine but a mutinous inner whispering. Verena in her heart wanted, I think, to come into the kitchen and be a part of it; but she was too like a lone man in a house full of women and children, and the only way she could make contact with us was through assertive outbursts: Dolly, get rid of that kitten, you want to aggravate my asthma? who left the water running in the bathroom? which one of you broke my umbrella? Her

ugly moods sifted through the house like a sour yellow mist.
That One. Hush now, hush.

Once a week, Saturdays mostly, we went to River Woods.
For these trips, which lasted the whole day, Catherine fried a
chicken and deviled a dozen eggs, and Dolly took along a choc-
olate layer cake and a supply of divinity fudge. Thus armed,
and carrying three empty grain sacks, we walked out the church
road past the cemetery and through the field of Indian grass.
Just entering the woods there was a double-trunked China
tree, really two trees, but their branches were so embraced
that you could step from one into the other; in fact, they were
bridged by a tree-house: spacious, sturdy, a model of a tree-
house, it was like a raft floating in the sea of leaves. The boys
who built it, provided they are still alive, must by now be very
old men; certainly the tree-house was fifteen or twenty years
old when Dolly first found it and that was a quarter of a cen-
tury before she showed it to me. To reach it was easy as climbing stairs; there were footholds of gnarled bark and tough vines
to grip; even Catherine, who was heavy around the hips and
complained of rheumatism, had no trouble. But Catherine felt
no love for the tree-house; she did not know, as Dolly knew
and made me know, that it was a ship, that to sit up there was
to sail along the cloudy coastline of every dream. Mark my
word, said Catherine, them boards are too old, them nails are
slippery as worms, gonna crack in two, gonna fall and bust our
heads don't I know it.

Storing our provisions in the tree-house, we separated into
the woods, each carrying a grain sack to be filled with herbs,
leaves, strange roots. No one, not even Catherine, knew altogether what went into the medicine, for it was a secret Dolly
kept to herself, and we were never allowed to look at the
gatherings in her own sack: she held tight to it, as though
inside she had captive a blue-haired child, a bewitched prince.
This was her story: "Once, back yonder when we were children (Verena still with her babyteeth and Catherine no higher
than a fence post) there were gipsies thick as birds in a blackberry patch—not like now, when maybe you see a few strag-
gling through each year. They came with spring: sudden, like
the dogwood pink, there they were—up and down the road and
in the woods around. But our men hated the sight of them, and
daddy, that was your great-uncle Uriah, said he would shoot
any he caught on our place. And so I never told when I saw
the gipsies taking water from the creek or stealing old winter
pecans off the ground. Then one evening, it was April and

falling rain, I went out to the cowshed where Fairybell had a
new little calf; and there in the cowshed were three gipsy
women, two of them old and one of them young, and the
young one was lying naked and twisting on the cornshucks.
When they saw that I was not afraid, that I was not going to
run and tell, one of the old women asked would I bring a light.
So I went to the house for a candle, and when I came back
the woman who had sent me was holding a red hollering baby
upside down by its feet, and the other woman was milking
Fairybell. I helped them wash the baby in the warm milk
and wrap it in a scarf. Then one of the old women took my
hand and said: Now I am going to give you a gift by teaching
you a rhyme. It was a rhyme about evergreen bark, dragon-
fly fern—and all the other things we come here in the woods
to find: *Boil till dark and pure if you want a dropsy cure*. In
the morning they were gone; I looked for them in the fields
and on the road; there was nothing left of them but the rhyme
in my head."

Calling to each other, hooting like owls loose in the daytime,
we worked all morning in opposite parts of the woods. Towards
afternoon, our sacks fat with skinned bark, tender, torn roots,
we climbed back into the green web of the China tree and
spread the food. There was good creek water in a mason jar,
or if the weather was cold a thermos of hot coffee, and we
wadded leaves to wipe our chicken-stained, fudge-sticky fingers.
Afterwards, telling fortunes with flowers, speaking of sleepy
things, it was as though we floated through the afternoon on
the raft in the tree; we belonged there, as the sun-silvered
leaves belonged, the dwelling whippoorwills.

About once a year I go over to the house on Talbo Lane, and
walk around in the yard. I was there the other day, and came
across an old iron tub lying overturned in the weeds like a
black fallen meteor: Dolly—Dolly, hovering over the tub drop-
ping our grain-sack gatherings into boiling water and stirring,
stirring with a sawed-off broomstick the brown as tobacco spit
brew. She did the mixing of the medicine alone while Catherine
and I stood watching like apprentices to a witch. We all helped
later with the bottling of it and, because it produced a fume
that exploded ordinary corks, my particular job was to roll
stoppers of toilet paper. Sales averaged around six bottles a
week, at two dollars a bottle. The money, Dolly said, belonged
to the three of us, and we spent it fast as it came in. We were
always sending away for stuff advertised in magazines: Take

Up Woodcarving, Parcheesi: the game for young and old, Anyone Can Play A Bazooka. Once we sent away for a book of
French lessons: it was my idea that if we got to talk French
we would have a secret language that Verena or nobody would
understand. Dolly was willing to try, but "Passez-moi a spoon"
was the best she ever did, and after learning "Je suis fatigué,"
Catherine never opened the book again: she said that was all
she needed to know.

Verena often remarked that there would be trouble if anyone ever got poisoned, but otherwise she did not show much
interest in the dropsy cure. Then one year we totaled up and
found we'd earned enough to have to pay an income tax.
Whereupon Verena began asking questions: money was like a
wildcat whose trail she stalked with a trained hunter's muffled
step and an eye for every broken twig. What, she wanted to
know, went into the medicine? and Dolly, flattered, almost
giggling, nonetheless waved her hands and said Well this and
that, nothing special.

Verena seemed to let the matter die; yet very often, sitting
at the supper table, her eyes paused ponderingly on Dolly, and
once, when we were gathered in the yard around the boiling
tub, I looked up and saw Verena in a window watching us
with uninterrupted fixity: by then, I suppose, her plan had
taken shape, but she did not make her first move until summer.

Twice a year, in January and again in August, Verena went
on buying trips to St. Louis or Chicago. That summer, the
summer I reached sixteen, she went to Chicago and after two
weeks returned accompanied by a man called Dr. Morris Ritz.
Naturally everyone wondered who was Dr. Morris Ritz? He
wore bow ties and sharp jazzy suits; his lips were blue and he
had gaudy small swerving eyes; altogether, he looked like a
mean mouse. We heard that he lived in the best room at the
Lola Hotel and ate steak dinners at Phil's Café. On the streets
he strutted along bobbing his shiny head at every passerby; he
made no friends, however, and was not seen in the company of
anyone except Verena, who never brought him to the house
and never mentioned his name until one day Catherine had the
gall to say, "Miss Verena, just who is this funny looking little
Dr. Morris Ritz?" and Verena, getting white around the
mouth, replied: "Well now, he's not half so funny looking as
some I could name."

Scandalous, people said, the way Verena was carrying on
with that little Jew from Chicago: and him twenty years
younger. The story that got around was that they were up to

something out in the old canning factory the other side of town. As it developed, they were; but not what the gang at the pool-hall thought. Most any afternoon you could see Verena and Dr. Morris Ritz walking out toward the canning factory, an abandoned blasted brick ruin with jagged windows and sagging doors. For a generation no one had been near it except school-kids who went there to smoke cigarettes and get naked to-gether. Then early in September, by way of a notice in the *Courier*, we learned for the first time that Verena had bought the old canning factory; but there was no mention as to what use she was planning to make of it. Shortly after this, Verena told Catherine to kill two chickens as Dr. Morris Ritz was coming to Sunday dinner.

During the years that I lived there, Dr. Morris Ritz was the only person ever invited to dine at the house on Talbo Lane. So for many reasons it was an occasion. Catherine and Dolly did a spring cleaning: they beat rugs, brought china from the attic, had every room smelling of floorwax and lemon polish. There was to be fried chicken and ham, English peas, sweet potatoes, rolls, banana pudding, two kinds of cake and tutti-frutti ice cream from the drugstore. Sunday noon Verena came in to look at the table: with its sprawling centerpiece of peach-colored roses and dense fancy stretches of silverware, it seemed set for a party of twenty; actually, there were only two places. Verena went ahead and set two more, and Dolly, seeing this, said weakly Well, it was all right if Collin wanted to eat at the table, but that she was going to stay in the kitchen with Cath-erine. Verena put her foot down: "Don't fool with me, Dolly. This is important. Morris is coming here expressly to meet you. And what-is more, I'd appreciate it if you'd hold up your head: it makes me dizzy, hanging like that."

Dolly was scared to death: she hid in her room, and long after our guest had arrived I had to be sent to fetch her. She was lying in the pink bed with a wet washrag on her forehead, and Catherine was sitting beside her. Catherine was all sleeked up, rouge on her cheeks like lollipops and her jaws jammed with more cotton than ever; she said, "Honey, you ought to get up from there—you're going to ruin that pretty dress." It was a calico dress Verena had brought from Chicago; Dolly sat up and smoothed it, then immediately lay down again: "If Verena knew how sorry I am," she said helplessly, and so I went and told Verena that Dolly was sick. Verena said she'd see about that, and marched off leaving me alone in the hall with Dr. Morris Ritz.

Oh he was a hateful thing. "So you're sixteen," he said, winking first one, then the other of his sassy eyes. "And throwing it around, huh? Make the old lady take you next time she goes to Chicago. Plenty of good stuff there to throw it at." He snapped his fingers and jiggled his razzle-dazzle, dagger-sharp shoes as though keeping time to some vaudeville tune: he might have been a tapdancer or a soda-jerk, except that he was carrying a brief case, which suggested a more serious occupation. I wondered what kind of doctor he was supposed to be; indeed, was on the point of asking when Verena returned steering Dolly by the elbow.

The shadows of the hall, the tapestried furniture failed to absorb her; without raising her eyes she lifted her hand, and Dr. Ritz gripped it so ruggedly, pumped it so hard she went nearly off balance. "Gee, Miss Talbo; am I honored to meet you!" he said, and cranked his bow tie.

We sat down to dinner, and Catherine came around with the chicken. She served Verena, then Dolly, and when the doctor's turn came he said, "Tell you the truth, the only piece of chicken I care about is the brain: don't suppose you'd have that back in the kitchen, mammy?"

Catherine looked so far down her nose she got almost cross-eyed; and with her tongue all mixed up in the cotton wadding she told him that, "Dolly's took those brains on her plate."

"These southern accents, Jesus," he said, genuinely dismayed.

"She says I have the brains on my plate," said Dolly, her cheeks red as Catherine's rouge. "But please let me pass them to you."

"If you're sure you don't mind . . ."

"She doesn't mind a bit," said Verena. "She only eats sweet things anyway. Here, Dolly: have some banana pudding."

Presently Dr. Ritz commenced a fit of sneezing. "The flowers, those roses, old allergy . . ."

"Oh dear," said Dolly who, seeing an opportunity to escape into the kitchen, seized the bowl of roses: it slipped, crystal crashed, roses landed in gravy and gravy landed on us all. "You see," she said, speaking to herself and with tears teetering in her eyes, "you see, it's hopeless."

"Nothing is hopeless, Dolly; sit down and finish your pudding," Verena advised in a substantial, chin-up voice. "Besides, we have a nice little surprise for you. Morris, show Dolly those lovely labels."

Murmuring "No harm done," Dr. Ritz stopped rubbing

gravy splotches off his sleeve, and went into the hall, returning with his brief case. His fingers buzzed through a sheaf of papers, then lighted on a large envelope which he passed down to Dolly.

There were gum-stickers in the envelope, triangular labels with orange lettering: Gipsy Queen Dropsy Cure: and a fuzzy picture of a woman wearing a bandana and gold earloops. "First class, huh?" said Dr. Ritz. "Made in Chicago. A friend of mine drew the picture: real artist, that guy," Dolly shuffled the labels with a puzzled, apprehensive expression until Verena asked: "Aren't you pleased?"

The labels twitched in Dolly's hands. "I'm not sure I understand."

"Of course you do," said Verena, smiling thinly. "It's obvious enough. I told Morris that old story of yours and he thought of this wonderful name."

"Gipsy Queen Dropsy Cure: very catchy, that," said the doctor. "Look great in ads."

"*My* medicine?" said Dolly, her eyes still lowered. "But I don't need any labels, Verena. I write my own."

Dr. Ritz snapped his fingers. "Say, that's good! We can have labels printed like her own handwriting: personal, see?"

"We've spent enough money already," Verena told him briskly; and, turning to Dolly, said: "Morris and I are going up to Washington this week to get a copyright on these labels and register a patent for the medicine—naming you as the inventor, naturally. Now the point is, Dolly, you must sit down and write out a complete formula for us."

Dolly's face loosened; and the labels scattered on the floor, skimmed. Leaning her hands on the table she pushed herself upward; slowly her features came together again, she lifted her head and looked blinkingly at Dr. Ritz, at Verena. "It won't do," she said quietly. She moved to the door, put a hand on its handle. "It won't do: because you haven't any right, Verena. Nor you, sir."

I helped Catherine clear the table: the ruined roses, the uncut cakes, the vegetables no one had touched. Verena and her guest had left the house together; from the kitchen window we watched them as they went toward town nodding and shaking their heads. Then we sliced the devil's-food cake and took it into Dolly's room.

Hush now! hush now! she said when Catherine began lighting into That One. But it was as though the rebellious inner

whispering had become a raucous voice, an opponent she must
outshout: Hush now! hush now! until Catherine had to put
her arms around Dolly and say hush, too.

We got out a deck of Rook cards and spread them on the
bed. Naturally Catherine had to go and remember it was Sunday; she said maybe we could risk another black mark in the
Judgment Book, but there were too many beside her name
already. After thinking it over, we told fortunes instead. Sometime around dusk Verena came home. We heard her footsteps in the hall; she opened the door without knocking, and
Dolly, who was in the middle of my fortune, tightened her
hold on my hand. Verena said: "Collin, Catherine, we will excuse you."

Catherine wanted to follow me up the ladder into the attic,
except she had on her fine clothes. So I went alone. There was
a good knothole that looked straight down into the pink room;
but Verena was standing directly under it, and all I could see
was her hat, for she was still wearing the hat she'd put on when
she left the house. It was a straw skimmer decorated with a
cluster of celluloid fruit. "Those are facts," she was saying,
and the fruit shivered, shimmered in the blue dimness. "Two
thousand for the old factory, Bill Tatum and four carpenters
working out there at eighty cents an hour, seven thousand
dollars worth of machinery already ordered, not to mention
what a specialist like Morris Ritz is costing. And why? All for
you!"

"All for me?" and Dolly sounded sad and failing as the dusk.
I saw her shadow as she moved from one part of the room to
another. "You are my own flesh, and I love you tenderly; in
my heart I love you. I could prove it now by giving you the
only thing that has ever been mine: then you would have it all.
Please, Verena," she said, faltering, "let this one thing belong
to me."

Verena switched on a light. "You speak of giving," and her
voice was hard as the sudden bitter glare. "All these years that
I've worked like a fieldhand: what haven't I given you? This
house, that . . ."

"You've given everything to me," Dolly interrupted softly.
"And to Catherine and to Collin. Except, we've earned our
way a bit: we've kept a nice home for you, haven't we?"

"Oh a fine home," said Verena, whipping off her hat. Her
face was full of blood. "You and that gurgling fool. Has it not
struck you that I never ask anyone into this house? And for a

very simple reason: I'm ashamed to. Look what happened today."

I could hear the breath go out of Dolly. "I'm sorry," she said faintly. "I am truly. I'd always thought there was a place for us here, that you needed us somehow. But it's going to be all right now, Verena. We'll go away."

Verena sighed. "Poor Dolly. Poor poor thing. Wherever would you go?"

The answer, a little while in coming, was fragile as the flight of a moth: "I know a place."

Later, I waited in bed for Dolly to come and kiss me good-night. My room, beyond the parlor in a faraway corner of the house, was the room where their father, Mr. Uriah Talbo, had lived. In his mad old age, Verena had brought him here from the farm, and here he'd died, not knowing where he was. Though dead ten, fifteen years, the pee and tobacco old-man smell of him still saturated the mattress, the closet, and on a shelf in the closet was the one possession he'd carried away with him from the farm, a small yellow drum: as a lad my own age he'd marched in a Dixie regiment rattling this little yellow drum, and singing. Dolly said that when she was a girl she'd liked to wake up winter mornings and hear her father singing as he went about the house building fires; after he was old, after he'd died, she sometimes heard his songs in the field of Indian grass. Wind, Catherine said; and Dolly told her: But the wind is us—it gathers and remembers all our voices, then sends them talking and telling through the leaves and the fields —I've heard Papa clear as day.

On such a night, now that it was September, the autumn winds would be curving through the taut red grass, releasing all the gone voices, and I wondered if he was singing among them, the old man in whose bed I lay falling asleep.

Then I thought Dolly at last had come to kiss me good-night, for I woke up sensing her near me in the room; but it was almost morning, beginning light was like a flowering foliage at the windows, and roosters ranted in distant yards. "Shhh, Collin," Dolly whispered, bending over me. She was wearing a woolen winter suit and a hat with a traveling veil that misted her face. "I only wanted you to know where we are going."

"To the tree-house?" I said, and thought I was talking in my sleep.

Dolly nodded. "Just for now. Until we know better what our plans will be." She could see that I was frightened, and put her hand on my forehead.

"You and Catherine: but not me?" and I was jerking with a chill. "You can't leave without me."

The town clock was tolling; she seemed to be waiting for it to finish before making up her mind. It struck five, and by the time the note had died away I had climbed out of bed and rushed into my clothes. There was nothing for Dolly to say except: "Don't forget your comb."

Catherine met us in the yard; she was crooked over with the weight of a brimming oilcloth satchel; her eyes were swollen, she had been crying, and Dolly, oddly calm and certain of what she was doing, said it doesn't matter, Catherine—we can send for your goldfish once we find a place. Verena's closed quiet windows loomed above us; we moved cautiously past them and silently out the gate. A fox terrier barked at us; but there was no one on the street, and no one saw us pass through the town except a sleepless prisoner gazing from the jail. We reached the field of Indian grass at the same moment as the sun. Dolly's veil flared in the morning breeze, and a pair of pheasants, nesting in our path, swept before us, their metal wings swiping the cockscomb-scarlet grass. The China tree was a September bowl of green and greenish gold: Gonna fall, gonna bust our heads, Catherine said, as all around us the leaves shook down their dew.

Two

I F IT hadn't been for Riley Henderson, I doubt anyone would have known, or at least known so soon, that we were in the tree.

Catherine had loaded her oilcloth satchel with the leftovers from Sunday dinner, and we were enjoying a breakfast of cake and chicken when gunfire slapped through the woods. We sat there with cake going dry in our mouths. Below, a sleek bird dog cantered into view, followed by Riley Henderson; he was shouldering a shotgun and around his neck there hung a garland of bleeding squirrels whose tails were tied together. Dolly lowered her veil, as though to camouflage herself among the leaves.

He paused not far away, and his wary, tanned young face tightened; propping his gun into position he took a roaming aim, as if waiting for a target to present itself. The suspense was too much for Catherine, who shouted: "Riley Henderson, don't you dare shoot us!"

His gun wavered, and he spun around, the squirrels swinging like a loose necklace. Then he saw us in the tree, and after a moment said, "Hello there, Catherine Creek; hello, Miss Talbo. What are you folks doing up there? Wildcat chase you?"

"Just sitting," said Dolly promptly, as though she were

afraid for either Catherine or I to answer. "That's a fine mess of squirrels you've got."

"Take a couple," he said, detaching two. "We had some for supper last night and they were real tender. Wait a minute, I'll bring them up to you."

"You don't have to do that; just leave them on the ground." But he said ants would get at them, and hauled himself into the tree. His blue shirt was spotted with squirrel blood, and flecks of blood glittered in his rough leather-colored hair; he smelled of gunpowder, and his homely well-made face was brown as cinnamon. "I'll be damned, it's a tree-house," he said, pounding his foot as though to test the strength of the boards. Catherine warned him that maybe it was a tree-house now, but it wouldn't be for long if he didn't stop that stamping. He said, "You build it, Collin?" and it was with a happy shock that I realized he'd called my name: I hadn't thought Riley Henderson knew me from dust. But I knew him, all right.

No one in our town ever had themselves so much talked about as Riley Henderson. Older people spoke of him with sighing voices, and those nearer his own age, like myself, were glad to call him mean and hard: that was because he would only let us envy him, would not let us love him, be his friend. Anyone could have told you the facts.

He was born in China, where his father, a missionary, had been killed in an uprising. His mother was from this town, and her name was Rose; though I never saw her myself, people say she was a beautiful woman until she started wearing glasses; she was rich too, having received a large inheritance from her grandfather. When she came back from China she brought Riley, then five, and two younger children, both girls; they lived with her unmarried brother, Justice of the Peace Horace Holton, a meaty spinsterish man with skin yellow as quince. In the following years Rose Henderson grew strange in her ways: she threatened to sue Verena for selling her a dress that shrank in the wash; to punish Riley, she made him hop on one leg around the yard reciting the multiplication table; otherwise, she let him run wild, and when the Presbyterian minister spoke to her about it she told him she hated her children and wished they were dead. And she must have meant it, for one Christmas morning she locked the bathroom door and tried to drown her two little girls in the tub: it was said that Riley broke the door down with a hatchet, which seems a tall order for a boy of nine or ten, whatever he was. Afterwards, Rose was sent off to a place on the Gulf Coast, an institution, and she may still be living there, at least I've never heard that she died. Now Riley and his uncle Horace Holton couldn't get on. One night he stole Horace's Oldsmobile and drove out to the Dance-N-Dine with Mamie Curtiss: she was fast as lightning, and maybe five years older than Riley, who was not more than fifteen at the time. Well, Horace heard they were at the Dance-N-Dine and got the Sheriff to drive him out there: he said he was going to teach Riley a lesson and have him arrested. But Riley said Sheriff, you're after the wrong party. Right there in front of a crowd he accused his uncle of stealing money that belonged to Rose and that was meant for him and his sisters. He offered to fight it out on the spot; and when Horace held back, he just walked over and socked him in the eye. The Sheriff put Riley in jail. But Judge Cool, an old friend of Rose's, began to investigate, and sure enough it turned out Horace had been draining Rose's money into his own account. So Horace simply packed his things and took the train to New Orleans where, a few months, later, we heard that, billed as the Minister of Romance, he had a job marrying couples on an excursion steamer that made moonlight cruises up the Mississippi. From then on, Riley was his own boss. With money borrowed against the inheritance he was coming into, he bought a red racy car and went skidding round the countryside with every floozy in town; the only nice girls you ever saw in that car were his sisters—he took them for a drive Sunday afternoons, a slow respectable circling of the square. They were pretty girls, his sisters, but they didn't have much fun, for he kept a strict watch, and boys were afraid to come near them. A reliable colored woman did their housework, otherwise they lived alone. One of his sisters, Elizabeth, was in my class at school, and she got the best grades, straight A's. Riley himself had quit school; but he was not one of the pool-hall loafs, nor did he mix with them; he fished in the daytime, or went hunting; around the old Holton house he made many improvements, as he was a good carpenter; and a good mechanic, too: for instance, he built a special car horn, it wailed like a train-whistle, and in the evening you could hear it howling as he roared down the road on his way to a dance in another town. How I longed for him to be my friend! and it seemed possible, he was just two years older. But I could remember the only time he ever spoke to me. Spruce in a pair of white flannels, he was off to a dance at the clubhouse, and he came into Verena's drugstore, where I sometimes helped out on Saturday nights. What he wanted was a package of Shadows, but I wasn't sure what Shadows were, so he had to come behind the counter and get them out of the drawer himself; and he laughed, not unkindly, though it was worse than if it had been: now he knew I was a fool, we would never be friends.

Dolly said, "Have a piece of cake, Riley," and he asked did we always have picnics this early in the day? then went on to say he considered it a fine idea: "Like swimming at night," he said. "I come down here while it's still dark, and go swimming in the river. Next time you have a picnic, call out so I'll know you're here."

"You are welcome any morning," said Dolly, raising her veil. "I daresay we will be here for some while."

Riley must have thought it a curious invitation, but he did not say so. He produced a package of cigarettes and passed it around; when Catherine took one, Dolly said: "Catherine Creek, you've never touched tobacco in your life." Catherine allowed as to how she may have been missing something: "It must be a comfort, so many folks speak in its favor; and Dolly-heart, when you get to be our age you've got to look for comforts." Dolly bit her lip; "Well, I don't suppose there's any harm," she said, and accepted a cigarette herself.

There are two things that will drive a boy crazy (according to Mr. Hand, who caught me smoking in the lavatory at school) and I'd given up one of them, cigarettes, two years before: not because I thought it would make me crazy, but because I thought it was imperiling my growth. Actually, now that I was a normal size, Riley was no taller than me, though he seemed to be, for he moved with the drawn-out cowboy awkwardness of a lanky man. So I took a cigarette, and Dolly, gushing un-inhaled smoke, said she thought we might as well all be sick together; but no one was sick, and Catherine said next time she would like to try a pipe, as they smelled so good. Whereupon Dolly volunteered the surprising fact that Verena smoked a pipe, something I'd never known: "I don't know whether she does any more, but she used to have a pipe and a can of Prince Albert with half an apple cut up in it. But you musn't tell that," she added, suddenly aware of Riley, who laughed aloud.

Usually, glimpsed on the street or seen passing in his car, Riley wore a tense, trigger-tempered expression; but there in the China tree he seemed relaxed: frequent smiles enriched his whole face, as though he wanted at least to be friendly, if not friends. Dolly, for her part, appeared to be at ease and en-joying his company. Certainly she was not afraid of him: perhaps it was because we were in the tree-house, and the tree-house was her own.

"Thank you for the squirrels, sir," she said, as he prepared to leave. "And don't forget to come again."

He swung himself to the ground. "Want a ride? My car's up by the cemetery."

Dolly told him: "That's kind of you; but really we haven't any place to go."

Grinning, he lifted his gun and aimed it at us; and Catherine yelled: You ought to be whipped, boy; but he laughed and waved and ran, his bird dog barking, booming ahead. Dolly said gaily, "Let's have a cigarette," for the package had been left behind.

By the time Riley reached town the news was roaring in the air like a flight of bees: how we'd run off in the middle of the night. Though neither Catherine nor I knew it, Dolly had left a note, which Verena found when she went for her morning coffee. As I understand it, this note simply said that we were going away and that Verena would not be bothered by us any more. She at once rang up her friend Morris Ritz at the Lola Hotel, and together they traipsed off to rouse the sheriff. It was Verena's backing that had put the sheriff into office; he was a fast-stepping, brassy young fellow with a brutal jaw and the bashful eyes of a cardsharp; his name was Junius Candle (can you believe it? the same Junius Candle who is a Senator today!). A searching party of deputies was gathered; telegrams were hurried off to sheriffs in other towns. Many years later, when the Talbo estate was being settled, I came across the handwritten original of this telegram—composed, I believe, by Dr. Ritz. *Be on lookout for following persons traveling together. Dolly Augusta Talbo, white, aged 60, yellow grayish hair, thin, height 5 feet 3, green eyes, probably insane but not likely to be dangerous, post description bakeries as she is cake eater. Catherine Creek, Negro, pretends to be Indian, age about 60, toothless, confused speech, short and heavy, strong, likely to be dangerous. Collin Talbo Fenwick, white, age 16, looks younger, height 5 feet 7, blond, gray eyes, thin, bad posture, scar at corner of mouth, surly natured. All three wanted as runaways.* They sure haven't run far, Riley said in the post office; and postmistress Mrs. Peters rushed to the telephone to say Riley Henderson had seen us in the woods below the cemetery.

While this was happening we were peaceably setting about

to make the tree-house cozy. From Catherine's satchel we took a rose and gold scrapquilt, and there was a deck of Rook cards, soap, rolls of toilet paper, oranges and lemons, candles, a frying pan, a bottle of blackberry wine, and two shoeboxes filled with food: Catherine bragged that she'd robbed the pantry of everything, leaving not even a biscuit for That One's breakfast.

Later, we all went to the creek and bathed our feet and faces in the cold water. There are as many creeks in River Woods as there are veins in a leaf: clear, crackling, they crook their way down into the little river that crawls through the woods like a green alligator. Dolly looked a sight, standing in the water with her winter suit-skirt hiked up and her veil pestering her like a cloud of gnats. I asked her, Dolly, why are you wearing that veil? and she said, "But isn't it proper for ladies to wear veils when they go traveling?"

Returning to the tree, we made a delicious jar of orangeade and talked of the future. Our assets were: forty-seven dollars in cash, and several pieces of jewelry, notably a gold fraternity ring Catherine had found in the intestines of a hog while stuffing sausages. According to Catherine, forty-seven dollars would buy us bus tickets anywhere: she knew somebody who had gone all the way to Mexico for fifteen dollars. Both Dolly and I were opposed to Mexico: for one thing, we didn't know the language. Besides, Dolly said, we shouldn't venture outside the state, and wherever we went it ought to be near a forest, otherwise how would we be able to make the dropsy cure? "To tell you the truth, I think we should set up right here in River Woods," she said, gazing about speculatively.

"In this old tree?" said Catherine. "Just put that notion out of your head, Dollyheart." And then: "You recall how we saw in the paper where a man bought a castle across the ocean and brought it every bit home with him? You recall that? Well, we maybe could put my little house on a wagon and haul it down here." But, as Dolly pointed out, the house belonged to Verena, and was therefore not ours to haul away. Catherine answered: "You wrong, sugar. If you feed a man, and wash his clothes, and born his children, you and that man are married, that man is yours. If you sweep a house, and tend its fires and fill its stove, and there is love in you all the years you are doing this, then you and that house are married, that house is yours. The way I see it, both those houses up there belong to us: in the eyes of God, we could put That One right out."

I had an idea: down on the river below us there was a for-saken houseboat, green with the rust of water, half-sunk; it had been the property of an old man who made his living catching catfish, and who had been run out of town after applying for a certificate to marry a fifteen-year-old colored girl. My idea was, why shouldn't we fix up the old houseboat and live there?

Catherine said that if possible she hoped to spend the rest of her life on land: "Where the Lord intended us," and she listed more of His intentions, one of these being that trees were meant for monkeys and birds. Presently she went silent and, nudging us, pointed in amazement down to where the woods opened upon the field of grass.

There, stalking toward us, solemnly, stiffly, came a distin-guished party: Judge Cool, the Reverend and Mrs. Buster, Mrs. Macy Wheeler; and leading them, Sheriff Junius Candle, who wore high-laced boots and had a pistol flapping on his hip. Sunmotes lilted around them like yellow butterflies, bram-bles brushed their starched town clothes, and Mrs. Macy Wheeler, frightened by a vine that switched against her leg, jumped back, screeching: I laughed.

And, hearing me, they looked up at us, an expression of perplexed horror collecting on some of their faces: it was as though they were visitors at a zoo who had wandered acci-dentally into one of the cages. Sheriff Candle slouched for-ward, his hand cocked on his pistol. He stared at us with puckered eyes, as if he were gazing straight into the sun. "Now look here . . ." he began, and was cut short by Mrs. Buster, who said: "Sheriff, we agreed to leave this to the Reverend." It was a rule of hers that her husband, as God's representative, should have first say in everything. The Reverend Buster cleared his throat, and his hands, as he rubbed them together, were like the dry scraping feelers of an insect. "Dolly Talbo," he said, his voice very fine-sounding for so stringy, stunted a man, "I speak to you on behalf of your sister, that good gra-cious woman . . ."

"That she is," sang his wife, and Mrs. Macy Wheeler par-roted her.

". . . who has this day received a grievous shock."

"That she has," echoed the ladies in their choir-trained voices.

Dolly looked at Catherine, touched my hand, as though asking us to explain what was meant by the group glowering below like dogs gathered around a tree of trapped possums. Inadvertently, and just, I think to have something in her hands, she picked up one of the cigarettes Riley had left.

"Shame on you," squalled Mrs. Buster, tossing her tiny baldish head: those who called her an old buzzard, and there were several, were not speaking of her character alone: in addition to a small vicious head, she had high hunched shoulders and a vast body. "I say shame on you. How can you have come so far from God as to sit up in a tree like a drunken Indian—sucking cigarettes like a common . . ."

"Floozy," supplied Mrs. Macy Wheeler.

". . . floozy, while your sister lies in misery flat on her back."

Maybe they were right in describing Catherine as dangerous, for she reared up and said: "Preacher lady, don't you go calling Dolly and us floozies; I'll come down there and slap you bowlegged." Fortunately, none of them could understand her; if they had, the sheriff might have shot her through the head: no exaggeration; and many of the white people in town would have said he did right.

Dolly seemed stunned, at the same time self-possessed. You see, she simply dusted her skirt and said: "Consider a moment, Mrs. Buster, and you will realize that we are nearer God than you—by several yards."

"Good for you, Miss Dolly. I call that a good answer." The man who had spoken was Judge Cool; he clapped his hands together and chuckled appreciatively. "Of course they are nearer God," he said, unfazed by the disapproving, sober faces around him. "They're in a tree, and we're on the ground."

Mrs. Buster whirled on him. "I'd thought you were a Christian, Charlie Cool. My ideas of a Christian do not include laughing at and encouraging a poor mad woman."

"Mind who you name as mad, Thelma," said the Judge. "That isn't especially Christian either."

The Reverend Buster opened fire. "Answer me this, Judge. Why did you come with us if it wasn't to do the Lord's will in a spirit of mercy?"

"The Lord's will?" said the Judge incredulously. "You don't know what that is any more than I do. Perhaps the Lord told these people to go live in a tree; you'll admit, at least, that He never told you to drag them out—unless, of course, Verena Talbo is the Lord, a theory several of you give credence to, eh Sheriff? No, sir, I did not come along to do anyone's will but my own: which merely means that I felt like taking a walk—

the woods are very handsome at this time of year." He picked
some brown violets and put them in his buttonhole.

"To hell with all that," began the Sheriff, and was again interrupted by Mrs. Buster, who said that under no circumstances would she tolerate swearing: Will we, Reverend? and
the Reverend, backing her up, said he'd be damned if they
would. "I'm in charge here," the Sheriff informed them,
thrusting his bully-boy jaw. "This is a matter for the law."

"Whose law, Junius?" inquired Judge Cool quietly. "Remember that I sat in the courthouse twenty-seven years, rather a
longer time than you've lived. Take care. We have no legal
right whatever to interfere with Miss Dolly."

Undaunted, the Sheriff hoisted himself a little into the tree.
"Let's don't have any more trouble," he said coaxingly, and
we could see his curved dog-teeth. "Come on down from there,
the pack of you." As we continued to sit like three nesting
birds he showed more of his teeth and, as though he were
trying to shake us out, angrily swayed a branch.

"Miss Dolly, you've always been a peaceful person," said
Mrs. Macy Wheeler. "Please come on home with us; you don't
want to miss your dinner." Dolly replied matter-of-factly that
we were not hungry: were they? "There's a drumstick for anybody that would like it."

Sheriff Candle said, "You make it hard on me, ma'am," and
pulled himself nearer. A branch, cracking under his weight,
sent through the tree a sad cruel thunder.

"If he lays a hand on any one of you, kick him in the head,"
advised Judge Cool. "Or I will," he said with sudden gallant
pugnacity: like an inspired frog he hopped and caught hold to
one of the Sheriff's dangling boots. The Sheriff, in turn,
grabbed my ankles, and Catherine had to hold me around the
middle. We were sliding, that we should all fall seemed inevi-
table, the strain was immense. Meanwhile, Dolly started pour-
ing what was left of our orangeade down the Sheriff's neck,
and abruptly, shouting an obscenity, he let go of me. They
crashed to the ground, the Sheriff on top of the Judge and the
Reverend Buster crushed beneath them both. Mrs. Macy
Wheeler and Mrs. Buster, augmenting the disaster, fell upon
them with crow-like cries of distress.

Appalled by what had happened, and the part she herself
had played, Dolly became so confused that she dropped the
empty orangeade jar: it hit Mrs. Buster on the head with a ripe
thud. "Beg pardon," she apologized, though in the furor no one
heard her.

When the tangle below unraveled, those concerned stood apart from each other embarrassedly, gingerly feeling of themselves. The Reverend looked rather flattened out, but no broken bones were discovered, and only Mrs. Buster, on whose skimpy-haired head a bump was pyramiding, could have justly complained of injury. She did so forthrightly. "You attacked me, Dolly Talbo, don't deny it, everyone here is a witness, everyone saw you aim that mason jar at my head. Junius, arrest her!"

The Sheriff, however, was involved in settling differences of his own. Hands on hips, swaggering, he bore down on the Judge, who was in the process of replacing the violets in his buttonhole. "If you weren't so old, I'd damn well knock you down."

"I'm not so old, Junius: just old enough to think men ought not to fight in front of ladies," said the Judge. He was a fair-sized man with strong shoulders and a straight body: though not far from seventy, he looked to be in his fifties. He clenched his fists and they were hard and hairy as coconuts. "On the other hand," he said grimly, "I'm ready if you are."

At the moment it looked like a fair enough match. Even the Sheriff seemed not so sure of himself; with diminishing bravado, he spit between his fingers, and said Well, nobody was going to accuse him of hitting an old man. "Or standing up to one," Judge Cool retorted. "Go on, Junius, tuck your shirt in your pants and trot along home."

The Sheriff appealed to us in the tree. "Save yourselves a lot of trouble: get out of there and come along with me now." We did not stir, except that Dolly dropped her veil, as though lowering a curtain on the subject once for all. Mrs. Buster, the lump on her head like a horn, said portentously, "Never mind, Sheriff. They've had their chance," and, eyeing Dolly, then the Judge, added: "You may imagine you are getting away with something. But let me tell you there will be a retribution —not in heaven, right here on earth."

"Right here on earth," harmonized Mrs. Macy Wheeler.

They left along the path, erect, haughty as a wedding procession, and passed into the sunlight where the red rolling grass swept up, swallowed them. Lingering under the tree, the Judge smiled at us and, with a small courteous bow, said: "Do I remember you offering a drumstick to anybody that would like it?"

He might have been put together from parts of the tree, for

his nose was like a wooden peg, his legs were strong as old roots, and his eyebrows were thick, tough as strips of bark. Among the topmost branches were beards of silvery moss the color of his center-parted hair, and the cowhide sycamore leaves, sifting down from a neighboring taller tree, were the color of his cheeks. Despite his canny, tomcat eyes, the general impression his face made was that of someone shy and countrified. Ordinarily he was not the one to make a show of himself, Judge Charlie Cool; there were many who had taken advantage of his modesty to set themselves above him. Yet none of them could have claimed, as he could, to be a graduate of Harvard University or to have twice traveled in Europe. Still, there were those who were resentful and felt that he put on airs: wasn't he supposed to read a page of Greek every morning before breakfast? and what kind of a man was it that would always have flowers in his buttonhole? If he wasn't stuck up, why, some people asked, had he gone all the way to Kentucky to find a wife instead of marrying one of our own women? I do not remember the Judge's wife; she died before I was old enough to be aware of her, therefore all that I repeat comes second-hand. So: the town never warmed up to Irene Cool, and apparently it was her own fault. Kentucky women are difficult to begin with, keyed-up, hellion-hearted, and Irene Cool, who was born a Todd in Bowling Green (Mary Todd, a second cousin once removed, had married Abraham Lincoln) let everyone around here know she thought them a backward, vulgar lot: she received none of the ladies of the town, but Miss Palmer, who did sewing for her, spread news of how she'd transformed the Judge's house into a place of taste and style with Oriental rugs and antique furnishings. She drove to and from Church in a Pierce-Arrow with all the windows rolled up, and in church itself she sat with a cologned handkerchief against her nose: *the smell of God ain't good enough for Irene Cool.* Moreover, she would not permit either of the local doctors to attend her family, this though she herself was a semi-invalid: a small backbone dislocation necessitated her sleeping on a bed of boards. There were crude jokes about the Judge getting full of splinters. Nevertheless, he fathered two sons, Todd and Charles Jr., both born in Kentucky where their mother had gone in order that they could claim to be natives of the bluegrass state. But those who tried to make out the Judge got the brunt of his wife's irritableness, that he was a miserable man, never had much of a case, and after she died even the hardest of their critics had to admit old Charlie must

surely have loved his Irene. For during the last two years of
her life, when she was very ill and fretful, he retired as cir-
cuit judge, then took her abroad to the places they had been
on their honeymoon. She never came back; she is buried in
Switzerland. Not so long ago Carrie Wells, a schoolteacher
here in town, went on a group tour to Europe; the only thing
connecting our town with that continent are graves, the graves
of soldier boys and Irene Cool; and Carrie, armed with a
camera for snapshots, set out to visit them all: though she
stumbled about in a cloud-high cemetery one whole afternoon,
she could not find the Judge's wife, and it is funny to think of
Irene Cool, serenely there on a mountain-side still unwilling
to receive. There was not much left for the Judge when he
came back; politicians like Meiself Tallsap and his gang had
come into power: those boys couldn't afford to have Charlie
Cool sitting in the courthouse. It was sad to see the Judge, a
fine-looking man dressed in narrowcut suits with a black silk
band sewn around his sleeve and a Cherokee rose in his buttonhole, sad to see him with nothing to do except go to the post
office or stop in at the bank. His sons worked in the bank,
prissy-mouthed, prudent men who might have been twins, for
they both were marshmallow-white, slump-shouldered, watery-
eyed. Charles Jr., he was the one who had lost his hair while
still in college, was vice-president of the bank, and Todd, the
younger son, was chief cashier. In no way did they resemble
their father, except that they had married Kentucky women.
These daughters-in-law had taken over the Judge's house and
divided it into two apartments with separate entrances; there
was an arrangement whereby the old man lived with first one
son's family, then the other. No wonder he'd felt like taking a
walk to the woods.

"Thank you, Miss Dolly," he said, wiping his mouth with
the back of his hand. "That's the best drumstick I've had since
I was a boy."

"It's the least we can do, a drumstick; you were very brave."
There was in Dolly's voice an emotional, feminine tremor that
struck me as unsuitable, not dignified; so, too, it must have
seemed to Catherine: she gave Dolly a reprimanding glance.
"Won't you have something more, a piece of cake?"

"No ma'm, thank you, I've had a sufficiency." He unloosened
from his vest a gold watch and chain, then lassoed the chain to
a strong twig above his head; it hung like a Christmas orna-
ment, and its feathery faded ticking might have been the heart-
beat of a delicate thing, a firefly, a frog. "If you can hear time

passing it makes the day last longer. I've come to appreciate a long day." He brushed back the fur of the squirrels, which lay curled in a corner as though they were only asleep. "Right through the head: good shooting, son."

Of course I gave the credit to the proper party. "Riley Henderson, was it?" said the Judge, and went on to say it was Riley who had let our whereabouts be known. "Before that, they must have sent off a hundred dollars' worth of telegrams," he told us, tickled at the thought. "I guess it was the idea of all that money that made Verena take to her bed."

Scowling, Dolly said, "It doesn't make a particle of sense, all of them behaving ugly that way. They seemed mad enough to kill us, though I can't see why, or what it has to do with Verena: she knew we were going away to leave her in peace, I told her, I even left a note. But if she's sick—is she, Judge? I've never known her to be."

"Never a day," said Catherine.

"Oh, she's upset all right," the Judge said with a certain contentment. "But Verena's not the woman to come down with anything an aspirin couldn't fix. I remember when she wanted to rearrange the cemetery, put up some kind of mausoleum to house herself and all you Talbos. One of the ladies around here came to me and said Judge, don't you think Verena Talbo is the most morbid person in town, contemplating such a big tomb for herself? and I said No, the only thing morbid was that she was willing to spend the money when not for an instant did she believe she was ever going to die."

"I don't like to hear talk against my sister," said Dolly curtly. "She's worked hard, she deserves to have things as she wants them. It's our fault, someway we failed her, there was no place for us in her house."

Catherine's cotton-wadding squirmed in her jaw like chewing tobacco. "Are you my Dollyheart? or some hypocrite? He's a friend, you ought to tell him the truth, how That One and the little Jew was stealing our medicine. . . ."

The Judge applied for a translation, but Dolly said it was simply nonsense, nothing worth repeating and, diverting him, asked if he knew how to skin a squirrel. Nodding dreamily, he gazed away from us, above us, his acornlike eyes scanning the sky-fringed, breeze-fooled leaves. "It may be that there is no place for any of us. Except we know there is, somewhere; and if we found it, but lived there only a moment, we could count ourselves blessed. This could be your place," he

said, shivering as though in the sky spreading wings had cast a
cold shade. "And mine."

Subtly as the gold watch spun its sound of time, the afternoon curved toward twilight. Mist from the river, autumn
haze, trailed moon-colors among the bronze, the blue trees,
and a halo, an image of winter, ringed the paling sun. Still the
Judge did not leave us: "Two women and a boy? at the mercy
of night? and Junius Candle, those fools up to God knows what?
I'm sticking with you." Surely, of the four of us, it was the
Judge who had most found his place in the tree. It was a pleasure to watch him, all twinkly as a hare's nose, and feeling himself a man again, more than that, a protector. He skinned the
squirrels with a jackknife, while in the dusk I gathered sticks
and built under the tree a fire for the frying pan. Dolly opened
the bottle of blackberry wine; she justified this by referring to
a chill in the air. The squirrels turned out quite well, very
tender, and the Judge said proudly that we should taste his
fried catfish sometime. We sipped the wine in silence; a smell
of leaves and smoke carrying from the cooling fire called up
thoughts of other autumns, and we sighed, heard, like sea-
roar, singings in the field of grass. A candle flickered in a
mason jar, and gipsy moths, balanced, blowing about the
flame, seemed to pilot its scarf of yellow among the black
branches.

There was, just then, not a footfall, but a nebulous sense
of intrusion: it might have been nothing more than the moon
coming out. Except there was no moon; nor stars. It was dark
as the blackberry wine. "I think there is someone—something
down there," said Dolly, expressing what we all felt.

The Judge lifted the candle. Night-crawlers slithered away
from its lurching light, a snowy owl flew between the trees.
"Who goes there?" he challenged with the conviction of a
soldier. "Answer up, who goes there?"

"Me, Riley Henderson." It was indeed. He separated from
the shadows, and his upraised, grinning face looked warped,
wicked in the candlelight. "Just thought I'd see how you were
getting on. Hope you're not sore at me: I wouldn't have told
where you were, not if I'd known what it was all about."

"Nobody blames you, son," said the Judge, and I remembered it was he who had championed Riley's cause against his
uncle Horace Holton: there was an understanding between
them. "We're enjoying a small taste of wine. I'm sure Miss
Dolly would be pleased to have you join us."

Catherine complained there was no room; another ounce,

and those old boards would give way. Still, we scrunched together to make a place for Riley, who had no sooner squeezed
into it than Catherine grabbed a fistful of his hair. "That's for
today with you pointing your gun at us like I told you not to;
and this," she said, yanking again and speaking distinctively
enough to be understood, "pays you back for setting the
Sheriff on us."

It seemed to me that Catherine was impertinent, but Riley
grunted good-naturedly, and said she might have better cause
to be pulling somebody's hair before the night was over. For
there was, he told us, excited feelings in the town, crowds like
Saturday night; the Reverend and Mrs. Buster especially were
brewing trouble: Mrs. Buster was sitting on her front porch
showing callers the bump on her head. Sheriff Candle, he said,
had persuaded Verena to authorize a warrant for our arrest
on the grounds that we had stolen property belonging to her.

"And Judge," said Riley, his manner grave, perplexed,
"they've even got the idea they're going to arrest you. Disturb-
ing the peace and obstructing justice, that's what I heard.
Maybe I shouldn't tell you this—but outside the bank I ran
into one of your boys, Todd. I asked him what he was going
to do about it, about them arresting you, I mean; and he said
Nothing, said they'd been expecting something of the kind,
that you'd brought it on yourself."

Leaning, the Judge snuffed out the candle; it was as though
an expression was occurring in his face which he did not want
us to see. In the dark one of us was crying, after a moment
we knew that it was Dolly, and the sound of her tears set off
silent explosions of love that, running the full circle round,
bound us each to the other. Softly, the Judge said: "When they
come we must be ready for them. Now, everybody listen to
me. . . ."

Three

W E MUST know our position to defend it; that is a primary rule. Therefore: what has brought us together? Trouble. Miss Dolly and her friends, they are in trouble. You, Riley: we both are in trouble. We belong in this tree or we wouldn't be here." Dolly grew silent under the confident sound of the Judge's voice; he said: "Today, when I started out with the Sheriff's party, I was a man convinced that his life will have passed uncommunicated and without trace. I think now that I will not have been so unfortunate. Miss Dolly, how long? fifty, sixty years? it was that far ago that I remember you, a stiff and blushing child riding to town in your father's wagon—never getting down from the wagon because you didn't want us town-children to see you had no shoes."

"They had shoes, Dolly and That One," Catherine muttered. "It was me that didn't have no shoes."

"All the years that I've seen you, never known you, not ever recognized, as I did today, what you are: a spirit, a pagan . . ."

"A pagan?" said Dolly, alarmed but interested.

"At least, then, a spirit, someone not to be calculated by the eye alone. Spirits are accepters of life, they grant its differences—and consequently are always in trouble. Myself, I

should never have been a Judge; as such, I was too often on
the wrong side: the law doesn't admit differences. Do you remember old Carper, the fisherman who had a houseboat on
the river? He was chased out of town—wanted to marry that
pretty little colored girl, I think she works for Mrs. Postum
now; and you know she loved him, I used to see them when I
went fishing, they were very happy together; she was to him
what no one has been to me, the one person in the world—
from whom nothing is held back. Still, if he had succeeded in
marrying her, it would have been the Sheriff's duty to arrest
and my duty to sentence him. I sometimes imagine all those
whom I've called guilty have passed the real guilt on to me:
it's partly that that makes me want once before I die to be
right on the right side."

"You on the right side now. That One and the Jew . . ."

"Hush," said Dolly.

"The one person in the world." It was Riley repeating the
Judge's phrase; his voice lingered inquiringly.

"I mean," the Judge explained, "a person to whom everything can be said. Am I an idiot to want such a thing? But ah,
the energy we spend hiding from one another, afraid as we
are of being identified. But here we are, identified: five fools
in a tree. A great piece of luck provided we know how to use
it: no longer any need to worry about the picture we present
—free to find out who we truly are. If we know that no one
can dislodge us; it's the uncertainty concerning themselves
that makes our friends conspire to deny the differences. By
scraps and bits I've in the past surrendered myself to strang-
ers—men who disappeared down the gangplank, got off at the
next station: put together, maybe they would've made the
one person in the world—but there he is with a dozen different faces moving down a hundred separate streets. This is my
chance to find that man—you are him, Miss Dolly, Riley, all
of you."

Catherine said, "I'm no man with any dozen faces: the notion," which irritated Dolly, who told her if she couldn't speak
respectably why not just go to sleep. "But Judge," said Dolly,
"I'm not sure I know what it is you have in mind we should
tell each other. Secrets?" she finished lamely.

"Secrets, no, no." The Judge scratched a match and re-
lighted the candle; his face sprang upon us with an expression
unexpectedly pathetic: we must help him, he was pleading.
"Speak of the night, the fact there is no moon. What one says
hardly matters, only the trust with which it is said, the sym-

pathy with which it is received. Irene, my wife, a remarkable
woman, we might have shared anything, and yet, yet nothing
in us combined, we could not touch. She died in my arms, and
at the last I said, Are you happy, Irene? have I made you
happy? Happy happy happy, those were her last words: equi-
vocal. I have never understood whether she was saying yes,
or merely answering with an echo: I should know if I'd ever
known her. My sons. I do not enjoy their esteem: I've wanted
it, more as a man than as a father. Unfortunately, they feel
they know something shameful about me. I'll tell you what
it is." His virile eyes, faceted with candle-glow, examined us
one by one, as though testing our attention, trust. "Five years
ago, nearer six, I sat down in a train-seat where some child
had left a child's magazine. I picked it up and was looking
through it when I saw on the back cover addresses of children
who wanted to correspond with other children. There was a
little girl in Alaska, her name appealed to me, Heather Falls.
I sent her a picture postcard; Lord, it seemed a harmless and
pleasant thing to do. She answered at once, and the letter
quite astonished me; it was a very intelligent account of life in
Alaska—charming descriptions of her father's sheep ranch, of
northern lights. She was thirteen and enclosed a photograph
of herself—not pretty, but a wise and kind looking child. I
hunted through some old albums, and found a Kodak made
on a fishing trip when I was fifteen—out in the sun and with
a trout in my hand: it looked new enough. I wrote her as
though I were still that boy, told her of the gun I'd got for
Christmas, how the dog had had pups and what we'd named
them, described a tent-show that had come to town. To be
growing up again and have a sweetheart in Alaska—well, it
was fun for an old man sitting alone listening to the noise of a
clock. Later on she wrote she'd fallen in love with a fellow she
knew, and I felt a real pang of jealousy, the way a youngster
would; but we have remained friends: two years ago, when I
told her I was getting ready for law school, she sent me a
gold nugget—it would bring me luck, she said." He took it
from his pocket and held it out for us to see: it made her come
so close, Heather Falls, as though the gently bright gift balanced in his palm was part of her heart.

"And that's what they think is shameful?" said Dolly, more
piqued than indignant. "Because you've helped keep company
a lonely little child in Alaska? It snows there so much."

Judge Cool closed his hand over the nugget. "Not that
they've mentioned it to me. But I've heard them talking at

night, my sons and their wives: wanting to know what to do
about me. Of course they'd spied out the letters. I don't believe in locking drawers—seems strange a man can't live without keys in what was at least once his own house. They think
it all a sign of . . ." He tapped his head.

"I had a letter once. Collin, sugar, pour me a taste," said
Catherine, indicating the wine. "Sure enough, I had a letter
once, still got it somewhere, kept it twenty years wondering
who was wrote it. Said Hello Catherine, come on to Miami
and marry with me, love Bill."

"Catherine. A man asked you to marry him—and you never
told one word of it to me?"

Catherine lifted a shoulder. "Well, Dollyheart, what was
the Judge saying? You don't tell anybody everything. Besides,
I've known a peck of Bills—wouldn't study marrying any of
them. What worries my mind is, which one of the Bills was it
wrote that letter? I'd like to know, seeing as it's the only letter
I ever got. It could be the Bill that put the roof on my house;
course, by the time the roof was up—my goodness, I have got
old, been a long day since I've given it two thoughts. There
was Bill that came to plow the garden, spring of 1913 it was;
that man sure could plow a straight row. And Bill that built
the chicken-coop: went away on a Pullman job; might have
been him wrote me that letter. Or Bill—uh uh, his name was
Fred—Collin, sugar, this wine is mighty good."

"I may have a drop more myself," said Dolly. "I mean,
Catherine has given me such a . . ."

"Hmn," said Catherine.

"If you spoke more slowly, or chewed less . . ." The Judge
thought Catherine's cotton was tobacco.

Riley had withdrawn a little from us; slumped over, he
stared stilly into the inhabited dark: I, I, I, a bird cried, "I—
you're wrong, Judge," he said.

"How so, son?"

The caught-up uneasiness that I associated with Riley
swamped his face. "I'm not in trouble: I'm nothing—or would
you call that my trouble? I lie awake thinking what do I know
how to do? hunt, drive a car, fool around; and I get scared
when I think maybe that's all it will ever come to. Another
thing, I've got no feelings—except for my sisters, which is
different. Take for instance, I've been going with this girl
from Rock City nearly a year, the longest time I've stayed with
one girl. I guess it was a week ago she flared up and said
where's your heart? said if I didn't love her she'd as soon die.

So I stopped the car on the railroad track; well, I said, let's just sit here, the Crescent's due in about twenty minutes. We didn't take our eyes off each other, and I thought isn't it mean that I'm looking at you and I don't feel anything except . . ."

"Except vanity?" said the Judge.

Riley did not deny it. "And if my sisters were old enough to take care of themselves, I'd have been willing to wait for the Crescent to come down on us."

It made my stomach hurt to hear him talk like that; I longed to tell him he was all I wanted to be.

"You said before about the one person in the world. Why couldn't I think of her like that? It's what I want, I'm no good by myself. Maybe, if I could care for somebody that way, I'd make plans and carry them out: buy that stretch of land past Parson's Place and build houses on it—I could do it if I got quiet."

Wind surprised, pealed the leaves, parted night clouds; showers of starlight were let loose: our candle, as though intimidated by the incandescence of the opening, star-stabbed sky, toppled, and we could see, unwrapped above us, a late wayaway wintery moon: it was like a slice of snow, near and far creatures called to it, hunched moon-eyed frogs, a claw-voiced wildcat. Catherine hauled out the rose scrapquilt, insisting Dolly wrap it around herself; then she tucked her arms around me and scratched my head until I let it relax on her bosom—You cold? she said, and I wiggled closer: she was good and warm as the old kitchen.

"Son, I'd say you were going at it the wrong end first," said the Judge, turning up his coat-collar. "How could you care about one girl? Have you ever cared about one leaf?"

Riley, listening to the wildcat with an itchy hunter's look, snatched at the leaves blowing about us like midnight butterflies; alive, fluttering as though to escape and fly, one stayed trapped between his fingers. The Judge, too: he caught a leaf; and it was worth more in his hand than in Riley's. Pressing it mildly against his cheek, he distantly said, "We are speaking of love. A leaf, a handful of seed—begin with these, learn a little what it is to love. First, a leaf, a fall of rain, then someone to receive what a leaf has taught you, what a fall of rain has ripened. No easy process, understand; it could take a lifetime, it has mine, and still I've never mastered it—I only know how true it is: that love is a chain of love, as nature is a chain of life."

"Then," said Dolly with an intake of breath, "I've been in

love all my life." She sank down into the quilt. "Well, no,"
and her voice fell off, "I guess not. I've never loved a," while
she searched for the word wind frolicked her veil, "gentleman.
You might say that I've never had the opportunity. Except
Papa," she paused, as though she'd said too much. A gauze of
starlight wrapped her closely as the quilt; something, the reciting frogs, the string of voices stretching from the field of
grass, lured, impelled her: "But I have loved everything else.
Like the color pink; when I was a child I had one colored
crayon, and it was pink; I drew pink cats, pink trees—for
thirty-four years I lived in a pink room. And the box I kept,
it's somewhere in the attic now, I must ask Verena please to
give it to me, it would be nice to see my first loves again:
what is there? a dried honeycomb, an empty hornet's nest,
other things, or an orange stuck with cloves and a jaybird's
egg—when I loved those love collected inside me so that it
went flying about like a bird in a sunflower field. But it's best
not to show such things, it burdens people and makes them, I
don't know why, unhappy. Verena scolds at me for what she
calls hiding in corners, but I'm afraid of scaring people if I
show that I care for them. Like Paul Jimson's wife; after he
got sick and couldn't deliver the papers any more, remember
she took over his route? poor thin little thing just dragging herself with that sack of papers. It was one cold afternoon, she
came up on the porch her nose running and tears of cold
hanging in her eyes—she put down the paper, and I said wait,
hold on, and took my handkerchief to wipe her eyes: I wanted
to say, if I could, that I was sorry and that I loved her—my
hand grazed her face, she turned with the smallest shout and
ran down the steps. Then on, she always tossed the papers from
the street, and whenever I heard them hit the porch it sounded
in my bones."

"Paul Jimson's wife: worrying yourself over trash like that!"
said Catherine, rinsing her mouth with the last of the wine.
"I've got a bowl of goldfish, just 'cause I like them don't make
me love the world. Love a lot of mess, my foot. You can talk
what you want, not going to do anything but harm, bringing
up what's best forgot. People ought to keep more things to
themselves. The deepdown ownself part of you, that's the good
part: what's left of a human being that goes around speaking
his privates? The Judge, he say we all up here 'cause of
trouble some kind. Shoot! We here for very plain reasons. One
is, this our tree-house, and two, That One and the Jew's trying
to steal what belongs to us. Three: you here, every one of you,

'cause you want to be: the deepdown part of you tells you so. This last don't apply to me. I like a roof over my own head. Dollyheart, give the Judge a portion of that quilt: man's shivering like was Halloween."

Shyly Dolly lifted a wing of the quilt and nodded to him; the Judge, not at all shy, slipped under it. The branches of the China tree swayed like immense oars dipping into a sea rolling and chilled by the far far stars. Left alone, Riley sat hunched up in himself like a pitiful orphan. "Snuggle up, hard head: you cold like anybody else," said Catherine, offering him the position on her right that I occupied on her left. He didn't seem to want to; maybe he noticed that she smelled like bitterweed, or maybe he thought it was sissy; but I said come on, Riley, Catherine's good and warm, better than a quilt. After a while Riley moved over to us. It was quiet for so long I thought everyone had gone to sleep. Then I felt Catherine stiffen. "It's just come to me who it was sent my letter: Bill Nobody. That One, that's who. Sure as my name's Catherine Creek she got some nigger in Miami to mail me a letter, thinking I'd scoot off there never to be heard from again." Dolly sleepily said hush now hush, shut your eyes: "Nothing to be afraid of; we've men here to watch out for us." A branch swung back, moonlight ignited the tree: I saw the Judge take Dolly's hand. It was the last thing I saw.

Four

Riley was the first to wake, and he wakened me. On the
skyline three morning stars swooned in the flush of an arriving
sun; dew tinseled the leaves, a jet chain of blackbirds swung
out to meet the mounting light. Riley beckoned for me to
come with him; we slid silently down through the tree. Catherine, snoring with abandon, did not hear us go; nor did Dolly
and the Judge who, like two children lost in a witch-ruled
forest, were asleep with their cheeks together.

We headed toward the river, Riley leading the way. The
legs of his canvas trousers whispered against each other. Every
little bit he stopped and stretched himself, as though he'd been
riding on a train. Somewhere we came to a hill of already
about and busy red ants. Riley unbuttoned his fly and began
to flood them; I don't know that it was funny, but I laughed to
keep him company. Naturally I was insulted when he switched
around and peed on my shoe. I thought it meant he had no
respect for me. I said to him why would he want to do a thing
like that? Don't you know a joke? he said, and threw a
hugging arm around my shoulder.

If such events can be dated, this I would say was the moment Riley Henderson and I became friends, the moment, at
least, when there began in him an affectionate feeling for me

47

that supported my own for him. Through brown briars under
brown trees we walked deep in the woods down to the river.
Leaves like scarlet hands floated on the green slow water.
A poking end of a drowned log seemed the peering head of
some river-beast. We moved on to the old houseboat, where
the water was clearer. The houseboat was slightly tipped over;
drifts of waterbay sheddings were like a rich rust on its roof
and declining deck. The inside cabin had a mystifying tended-
to look. Scattered around were issues of an adventure magazine, there was a kerosene lamp and a line of beer empties
ranged on a table; the bunk sported a blanket, a pillow, and
the pillow was colored with pink markings of lipstick. In a
rush I realized the houseboat was someone's hide-out; then,
from the grin taking over Riley's homely face, I knew whose
it was. "What's more," he said, "you can get in a little fishing
on the side. Don't you tell anybody." I crossed an admiring
heart.

While we were undressing I had a kind of dream. I dreamed
the houseboat had been launched on the river with the five of
us aboard: our laundry flapped like sails, in the pantry a coco-
nut cake was cooking, a geranium bloomed on the windowsill
—together we floated over changing rivers past varying views.

The last of summer warmed the climbing sun, but the water,
at first plunge, sent me chattering and chicken-skinned back
to the deck where I stood watching Riley unconcernedly propel
himself to and fro between the banks. An island of bamboo
reeds, standing like the legs of cranes, shivered in a shallow
patch, and Riley waded out among them with lowered, hunting
eyes. He signaled to me. Though it hurt, I eased down into the
cold river and swam to join him. The water bending the bamboo was clear and divided into knee-deep basins—Riley hovered above one: in the thin pool a coal-black catfish lay doz-
ingly trapped. We closed in upon it with fingers tense as fork-
prongs: thrashing backwards, it flung itself straight into my
hands. The flailing razory whiskers made a gash across my
palm, still I had the sense to hold on—thank goodness, for it's
the only fish I ever caught. Most people don't believe it when
I tell about catching a catfish barehanded; I say well ask Riley
Henderson. We drove a spike of bamboo through its gills and
swam back to the houseboat holding it aloft. Riley said it was
one of the fattest catfish he'd ever seen: we would take it
back to the tree and, since he'd bragged what a great hand he
was at frying a catfish, let the Judge fix it for breakfast. As it
turned out, that fish never got eaten.

All this time at the tree-house there was a terrible situation. During our absence Sheriff Candle had returned backed by deputies and a warrant of arrest. Meanwhile, unaware of what was in store, Riley and I lazed along kicking over toadstools, sometimes stopping to skip rocks on the water.

We still were some distance away when rioting voices reached us; they rang in the trees like axe-blows. I heard Catherine scream: roar, rather. It made such soup of my legs I couldn't keep up with Riley, who grabbed a stick and began to run. I zigged one way, zagged another, then, having made a wrong turn, came out on the grass-field's rim. And there was Catherine.

Her dress was ripped down the front: she was good as naked. Ray Oliver, Jack Mill, and Big Eddie Stover, three grown men, cronies of the Sheriff, were dragging and slapping her through the grass. I wanted to kill them; and Catherine was trying to: but she didn't stand a chance—though she butted them with her head, bounced them with her elbows. Big Eddie Stover was legally born a bastard; the other two made the grade on their own. It was Big Eddie that went for me, and I slammed my catfish flat in his face. Catherine said, "You leave my baby be, he's an orphan"; and, when she saw that he had me around the waist: "In the booboos, Collin, kick his old booboos." So I did. Big Eddie's face curdled like clabber. Jack Mill (he's the one who a year later got locked in the ice-plant and froze to death: served him right) snatched at me, but I bolted across the field and crouched down in the tallest grass. I don't think they bothered to look for me, they had their hands so full with Catherine; she fought them the whole way, and I watched her, sick with knowing there was no help to give, until they passed out of sight over the ridge into the cemetery.

Overhead two squawking crows crossed, recrossed, as though making an evil sign. I crept toward the woods—near me, then, I heard boots cutting through the grass. It was the Sheriff; with him was a man called Will Harris. Tall as a door, buffalo-shouldered, Will Harris had once had his throat eaten out by a mad dog; the scars were bad enough, but his damaged voice was worse: it sounded giddy and babyfied, like a midget's. They passed so close I could have untied Will's shoes. His tiny voice, shrilling at the Sheriff, jumped with Morris Ritz's name and Verena's: I couldn't make out exactly, except something had happened about Morris Ritz and Verena had sent Will to bring back the Sheriff. The Sheriff said: "What in hell does the woman want, an army?" When they were gone I sprang up and ran into the woods.

In sight of the China tree I hid behind a fan of fern: I thought one of the Sheriff's men might still be hanging around. But there was nothing, simply a lonely singing bird. And no one in the tree-house: smoky as ghosts, streamers of sunlight illuminated its emptiness. Numbly I moved into view and leaned my head against the tree's trunk; at this, the vision of the houseboat returned: our laundry flapped, the geranium bloomed, the carrying river carried us out to sea into the world.

"Collin." My name fell out of the sky. "Is that you I hear? are you crying?"

It was Dolly, calling from somewhere I could not see— until, climbing to the tree's heart, I saw in the above distance Dolly's dangling childish shoe. "Careful boy," said the Judge, who was beside her, "you'll shake us out of here." Indeed, like gulls resting on a ship's mast, they were sitting in the absolute tower of the tree; afterwards, Dolly was to remark that the view afforded was so enthralling she regretted not having visited there before. The Judge, it developed, had seen the approach of the Sheriff and his men in time for them to take refuge in those heights. "Wait, we're coming," she said; and, with one arm steadied by the Judge, she descended like a fine lady sweeping down a flight of stairs.

We kissed each other; she continued to hold me. "She went to look for you—Catherine; we didn't know where you were, and I was so afraid, I . . ." Her fear tingled my hands: she felt like a shaking small animal, a rabbit just taken from the trap. The Judge looked on with humbled eyes, fumbling hands; he seemed to feel in the way, perhaps because he thought he'd failed us in not preventing what had happened to Catherine. But then, what could he have done? Had he gone to her aid he would only have got himself caught: they weren't fooling, the Sheriff, Big Eddie Stover and the others. I was the one to feel guilty. If Catherine hadn't gone to look for me they probably never would have caught her. I told of what had taken place in the field of grass.

But Dolly really wanted not to hear. As thought scattering a dream she brushed back her veil. "I want to believe Catherine is gone: and I can't. If I could I would run to find her. I want to believe Verena has done this: and I can't. Collin, what do you think: is it that after all the world is a bad place? Last night I saw it so differently."

The Judge focused his eyes on mine: he was trying, I think, to tell me how to answer. But I knew myself. No matter what passions compose them, all private worlds are good, they are never vulgar places: Dolly had been made too civilized by her own, the one she shared with Catherine and me, to feel the winds of wickedness that circulate elsewhere: No, Dolly, the world is not a bad place. She passed a hand across her forehead: "If you are right, then in a moment Catherine will be walking under the tree— she won't have found you or Riley, but she will have come back."

"By the way," said the Judge, "where *is* Riley?"

He'd run ahead of me, that was the last I'd seen of him; with an anxiety that struck us simultaneously, the Judge and I stood up and started yelling his name. Our voices, curving slowly around the woods, again, again swung back on silence. I knew what had happened: he'd fallen into an old Indian well —many's the case I could tell you of. I was about to suggest this when abruptly the Judge put a finger to his lips. The man must have had ears like a dog: I couldn't hear a sound. But he was right, there was someone on the path. It turned out to be Maude Riordan and Riley's older sister, the smart one, Elizabeth. They were very dear friends and wore white matching sweaters. Elizabeth was carrying a violin case.

"Look here, Elizabeth," said the Judge, startling the girls, for as yet they had not discovered us. "Look here, child, have you seen your brother?"

Maude recovered first, and it was she who answered. "We sure have," she said emphatically. "I was walking Elizabeth home from her lesson when Riley came along doing ninety miles an hour; nearly ran us over. You should speak to him, Elizabeth. Anyway, he asked us to come down here and tell you not to worry, said he'd explain everything later. Whatever that means."

Both Maude and Elizabeth had been in my class at school; they'd jumped a grade and graduated the previous June. I knew Maude especially well because for a summer I'd taken piano lessons from her mother; her father taught violin, and Elizabeth Henderson was one of his pupils. Maude herself played the violin beautifully; just a week before I'd read in the town paper where she'd been invited to play on a radio program in Birmingham: I was glad to hear it. The Riordans were nice people, considerate and cheerful. It was not because I wanted to learn piano that I took lessons with Mrs. Riordan— rather, I liked her blond largeness, the sympathetic, educated

talk that went on while we sat before the splendid upright that
smelled of polish and attention; and what I particularly liked
was afterwards, when Maude would ask me to have a lemon-
ade on the cool back porch. She was snub-nosed and elfin-
eared, a skinny excitable girl who from her father had in-
herited Irish black eyes and from her mother platinum hair
pale as morning—not the least like her best friend, the soulful
and shadowy Elizabeth. I don't know what those two talked
about, books and music maybe. But with me Maude's sub-
jects were boys, dates, drugstore slander: didn't I think it was
terrible, the awful girls Riley Henderson chased around with?
she felt so sorry for Elizabeth, and thought it wonderful how,
despite all, Elizabeth held up her head. It didn't take a genius
to see that Maude was heartset on Riley; nevertheless, I imagined for a while that I was in love with her. At home I kept
mentioning her until finally Catherine said Oh Maude Riordan,
she's too scrawny—nothing on her to pinch, a man's crazy to
give her the time of day. Once I showed Maude a big evening,
made for her with my own hands a sweet-pea corsage, then
took her to Phil's Café where we had Kansas City steaks; afterwards, there was a dance at the Lola Hotel. Still she behaved
as though she hadn't expected to be kissed good night. "I
don't think that's necessary, Collin—though it was cute of you
to take me out." I was let down, you can see why; but as I
didn't allow myself to brood over it our friendship went on
little changed. One day, at the end of a lesson, Mrs. Riordan
omitted the usual new piece for home practice; instead, she
kindly informed me that she preferred not to continue with
my lessons: "We're very fond of you, Collin, I don't have to
say that you're welcome in this house at any time. But dear,
the truth is you have no ability for music; it happens that way
occasionally, and I don't think it's fair on either of us to pretend otherwise." She was right, all the same my pride was
hurt, I couldn't help feeling pushed-out, it made me miserable
to think of the Riordans, and gradually, in about the time it
took to forget my few hard-learned tunes, I drew a curtain
on them. At first Maude used to stop me after school and ask
me over to her house; one way or another I always got out
of it; furthermore, it was winter then and I liked to stay in the
kitchen with Dolly and Catherine. Catherine wanted to know:
How come you don't talk any more about Maude Riordan? I
said because I don't, that's all. But while I didn't talk, I must
have been thinking; at least, seeing her there under the tree,
old feelings squeezed my chest. For the first time I considered

the circumstances self-consciously: did we, Dolly, the Judge and I, strike Maude and Elizabeth as a ludicrous sight? I could be judged by them, they were my own age. But from their manner we might just have met on the street or at the drugstore.

The Judge said, "Maude, how's your daddy? Heard he hasn't been feeling too good."

"He can't complain. You know how men are, always looking for an ailment. And yourself, sir?"

"That's a pity," said the Judge, his mind wandering. "You give your daddy my regards, and tell him I hope he feels better."

Maude submitted agreeably: "I will, sir, thank you. I know he'll appreciate your concern." Draping her skirt, she dropped on the moss and settled beside her an unwilling Elizabeth. For Elizabeth no one used a nickname; you might begin by calling her Betty, but in a week it would be Elizabeth again: that was her effect. Languid, banana-boned, she had dour black hair and an apathetic, at moments saintly face—in an enamel locket worn around her lily-stalk neck she preserved a miniature of her missionary father. "Look, Elizabeth, isn't that a becoming hat Miss Dolly has on? Velvet, with a veil."

Dolly roused herself; she patted her head. "I don't generally wear hats—we intended to travel."

"We heard you'd left home," said Maude; and, proceeding more frankly: "In fact that's all anyone talks about, isn't it, Elizabeth?" Elizabeth nodded without enthusiasm. "Gracious, there are some peculiar stories going around. I mean, on the way here we met Gus Ham and he said that colored woman Catherine Crook (is that her name?) had been arrested for hitting Mrs. Buster with a mason jar."

In sloping tones, Dolly said, "Catherine—had nothing to do with it."

"I guess someone did," said Maude. "We saw Mrs. Buster in the post office this morning; she was showing everybody a bump on her head, quite large. It looked genuine to us, didn't it Elizabeth?" Elizabeth yawned. "To be sure, I don't care who hit her, I think they ought to get a medal."

"No," sighed Dolly, "it isn't proper, it shouldn't have happened. We all will have a lot to be sorry for."

At last Maude took account of me. "I've been wanting to see you, Collin," she said hurrying as though to hide an embarrassment: mine, not hers. "Elizabeth and I are planning a Halloween party, a real scary one, and we thought it would be grand to dress you in a skeleton suit and sit you in a dark room to tell people's fortunes: because you're so good at . . ."

"Fibbing," said Elizabeth disinterestedly.

"Which is what fortune-telling is," Maude elaborated.

I don't know what gave them the idea I was such a story-teller, unless it was at school I'd shown a superior talent for alibis. I said it sounded fine, the party. "But you better not count on me. We might be in jail by then."

"Oh well, in that case," said Maude, as if accepting one of my old and usual excuses for not coming to her house.

"Say, Maude," said the Judge, helping us out of the silence that had fallen, "you're getting to be a celebrity: I saw in the paper where you're going to play on the radio."

As though dreaming aloud, she explained the broadcast was the finals of a state competition; if she won, the prize was a musical scholarship at the University: even second prize meant a half-scholarship. "I'm going to play a piece of daddy's, a serenade: he wrote it for me the day I was born. But it's a surprise, I don't want him to know."

"Make her play it for you," said Elizabeth, unclasping her violin case.

Maude was generous, she did not have to be begged. The wine-colored violin, coddled under her chin, trilled as she tuned it; a brazen butterfly, lighting on the bow, was spiraled away as the bow swept across the strings singing a music that seemed a blizzard of butterflies flying, a sky-rocket of spring sweet to hear in the gnarled fall woods. It slowed, saddened, her silver hair drooped across the violin. We applauded; after we'd stopped there went on sounding a mysterious extra pair of hands. Riley stepped from behind a bank of fern, and when she saw him Maude's cheeks pinked. I don't think she would have played so well if she'd known he was listening.

Riley sent the girls home; they seemed reluctant to go, but Elizabeth was not used to disobeying her brother. "Lock the doors," he told her, "and Maude, I'd appreciate it if you'd spend the night at our place: anybody comes by asking for me, say you don't know where I am."

I had to help him into the tree, for he'd brought back his gun and a knapsack heavy with provisions—a bottle of rose and raisin wine, oranges, sardines, wieners, rolls from the Katydid Bakery, a jumbo box of animal crackers: each item appearing stepped up our spirits, and Dolly, overcome by the animal crackers, said Riley ought to have a kiss.

But it was with grave face that we listened to his report.

When we'd separated in the woods it was toward the sound of Catherine that he'd run. This had brought him to the grass: he'd been watching when I had my encounter with Big Eddie Stover. I said well why didn't you help me? "You were doing all right: I don't figure Big Eddie's liable to forget you too soon: poor fellow limped along doubled over." Besides, it occurred to him that no one knew he was one of us, that he'd joined us in the tree: he was right to have stayed hidden, it made it possible for him to follow Catherine and the deputies into town. They'd stuffed her into the rumble-seat of Big Eddie's old coupé and driven straight to jail: Riley trailed them in his car. "By the time we reached the jail she seemed to have got quieted down; there was a little crowd hanging around, kids, some old farmers—you would have been proud of Catherine, she walked through them holding her dress together and her head like this." He tilted his head at a royal angle. How often I'd seen Catherine do that, especially when anyone criticized her (for hiding puzzle pieces, spreading misinformation, not having her teeth fixed); and Dolly, recognizing it too, had to blow her nose. "But," said Riley, "as soon as she was inside the jail she kicked up another fuss." In the jail there are only four cells, two for colored and two for white. Catherine had objected to being put in a colored people's cell.

The Judge stroked his chin, waved his head. "You didn't get a chance to speak to her? She ought to have had the comfort of knowing one of us was there."

"I stood around hoping she'd come to the window. But then I heard the other news."

Thinking back, I don't see how Riley could have waited so long to tell us. Because, my God: our friend from Chicago, that hateful Dr. Morris Ritz, had skipped town after rifling Verena's safe of twelve thousand dollars in negotiable bonds and more than seven hundred dollars in cash: that, as we later learned, was not half his loot. But wouldn't you know? I realized this was what baby-voiced Will Harris had been recounting to the Sheriff: no wonder Verena had sent a hurry call: her troubles with us must have become quite a side issue. Riley had a few details: he knew that Verena, upon discovering the safe door swung open (this happened in the office she kept above her drygoods store) had whirled around the corner to the Lola Hotel, there to find that Morris Ritz had checked out the previous evening: she fainted: when they revived her she fainted all over again.

Dolly's soft face hollowed; an urge to go to Verena was rising, at the same moment some sense of self, a deeper will, held her. Regretfully she gazed at me. "It's better you know it now, Collin; you shouldn't have to wait until you're as old as I am: the world is a bad place."

A change, like a shift of wind, overcame the Judge: he looked at once his age, autumnal, bare, as though he believed that Dolly, by accepting wickedness, had forsaken him. But I knew she had not: he'd called her a spirit, she was really a woman. Uncorking the rose and raisin wine, Riley spilled its topaz color into four glasses; after a moment he filled a fifth, Catherine's. The Judge, raising the wine to his lips, proposed a toast: "To Catherine, give her trust." We lifted our glasses, and "Oh Collin," said Dolly, a sudden stark thought widening her eyes, "you and I, we're the only ones that can understand a word she says!"

Five

THE following day, which was the first of October, a Wednesday, is one day I won't forget.

First off, Riley woke me by stepping on my fingers. Dolly, already awake, insisted I apologize for cursing him. Courtesy, she said, is more important in the morning than at any other time: particularly when one is living in such close quarters. The Judge's watch, still bending the twig like a heavy gold apple, gave the time as six after six. I don't know whose idea it was, but we breakfasted on oranges and animal crackers and cold hotdogs. The Judge grouched that a body didn't feel human till he'd had a pot of hot coffee. We agreed that coffee was what we all most missed. Riley volunteered to drive into town and get some; also, he would have a chance to scout around, find out what was going on. He suggested I come with him: "Nobody's going to see him, not if he stays down in the seat." Although the Judge objected, saying he thought it foolhardy, Dolly could tell I wanted to go: I'd yearned so much for a ride in Riley's car that now the opportunity presented itself nothing, even the prospect that no one might see me, could have thinned my excitement. Dolly said, "I can't see there's any harm. But you ought to have a clean shirt: I could plant turnips in the collar of that one."

The field of grass was without voice, no pheasant rustle,

furtive flurry; the pointed leaves were sharp and blood-red as the aftermath arrows of a massacre; their brittleness broke beneath our feet as we waded up the hill into the cemetery. The view from there is very fine: the limitless trembling surface of River Woods, fifty unfolding miles of ploughed, wind-milled farmland, far-off the spired courthouse tower, smoking chimneys of town. I stopped by the graves of my mother and father. I had not often visited them, it depressed me, the tomb-cold stone—so unlike what I remembered of them, their aliveness, how she'd cried when he went away to sell his frigidaires, how he'd run naked into the street. I wanted flowers for the terracotta jars sitting empty on the streaked and muddied marble. Riley helped me; he tore beginning buds off a japonica tree, and watching me arrange them, said: "I'm glad your ma was nice. Bitches, by and large." I wondered if he meant his own mother, poor Rose Henderson, who used to make him hop around the yard reciting the multiplication table. It did seem to me, though, that he'd made up for those hard days. After all, he had a car that was supposed to have cost three thousand dollars. Second-hand, mind you. It was a foreign car, an Alfa-Romeo roadster (Romeo's Alfa, the joke was) he'd bought in New Orleans from a politician bound for the penitentiary.

As we purred along the unpaved road toward town I kept hoping for a witness: there were certain persons it would have done my heart good to have seen me sailing by in Riley Henderson's car. But it was too early for anyone much to be about; breakfast was still on the stove, and smoke soared out the chimneys of passing houses. We turned the corner by the church, drove around the square and parked in the dirt lane that runs between Cooper's Livery and the Katydid Bakery. There Riley left me with orders to stay put: he wouldn't be more than an hour. So, stretching out on the seat, I listened to the chicanery of thieving sparrows in the livery stable's haystacks, breathed the fresh bread, tart as currant odors escaping from the bakery. The couple who owned this bakery, County was their name, Mr. and Mrs. C. C. County, had to begin their day at three in the morning to be ready by opening time, eight o'clock. It was a clean prosperous place. Mrs. County could afford the most expensive clothes at Verena's drygoods store. While I lay there smelling the good things, the back door of the bakery opened and Mr. County, broom in hand, swept flour dust into the lane. I guess he was surprised to see Riley's car, and surprised to find me in it.

"What you up to, Collin?"

"Up to nothing, Mr. County," I said, and asked myself if he knew about our trouble.

"Sure am happy October's here," he said, rubbing the air with his fingers as though the chill woven into it was a material he could feel. "We have a terrible time in the summer: ovens and all make it too hot to live. See here, son, there's a gingerbread man waiting for you—come on in and run him down."

Now he was not the kind of man to get me in there and then call the Sheriff.

His wife welcomed me into the spiced heat of the oven room as though she could think of nothing pleasanter than my being there. Most anyone would have liked Mrs. County. A chunky woman with no fuss about her, she had elephant ankles, developed arms, a muscular face permanently fire-flushed; her eyes were like blue cake-icing, her hair looked as if she'd mopped it around in a flour barrel, and she wore an apron that trailed to the tips of her toes. Her husband also wore one; sometimes, with the fulsome apron still tied around him, I'd seen him crossing the street to have a time-off beer with the men that lean around the corner at Phil's Café: he seemed a painted clown, flopping, powdered, elegantly angular.

Clearing a place on her work table, Mrs. County set me down to a cup of coffee and a warm tray of cinnamon rolls, the kind Dolly relished. Mr. County suggested I might prefer something else: "I promised him, what did I promise? a gingerbread man." His wife socked a lump of dough: "Those are for kids. He's a grown man; or nearly. Collin, just how old are you?"

"Sixteen."

"Same as Samuel," she said, meaning her son, whom we all called Mule: inasmuch as he was not much brighter than one. I asked what was their news of him? because the previous autumn, after having been left back in the eighth grade three years running, Mule had gone to Pensacola and joined the Navy. "He's in Panama, last we heard," she said, flattening the dough into a piecrust. "We don't hear often. I wrote him once, I said Samuel you do better about writing home or I'm going to write the President exactly how old you are. Because you know he joined up under false pretenses. I was darned mad at the time—blamed Mr. Hand up at the schoolhouse: that's why Samuel did it, he just couldn't tolerate always being left behind in the eighth grade, him getting so tall and the other children so little. But now I can see Mr. Hand was right: it wouldn't be fair to the rest of you boys if they promoted Samuel when he didn't do his work proper. So maybe it turned out for the best. C. C., show Collin the picture."

Photographed against a background of palms and real sea, four smirking sailors stood with their arms linked together; underneath was written, God Bless Mom and Pop, Samuel. It rankled me. Mule, off seeing the world, while I, well, maybe I deserved a gingerbread man. As I returned the picture, Mr. County said: "I'm all for a boy serving his country. But the bad part of it is, Samuel was just getting where he could give us a hand around here. I sure hate to depend on nigger help. Lying and stealing, never know where you are."

"It beats me why C.C. carries on like that," said his wife, knotting her lips. "He knows it irks me. Colored people are no worse than white people: in some cases, better. I've had occasion to say so to other people in this town. Like this business about old Catherine Creek. Makes me sick. Cranky she may be, and peculiar, but there's as good a woman as you'll find. Which reminds me, I mean to send her a dinner-tray up to the jail, for I'll wager the Sheriff doesn't set much of a table."

So little, once it has changed, changes back: the world knew us: we would never be warm again: I let go, saw winter coming toward a cold tree, cried, cried, came apart like a rain-rotted rag. I'd wanted to since we left the house. Mrs. County begged pardon if she'd said anything to upset me; with her kitchen-slopped apron she wiped my face, and we laughed, had to, at the mess it made, the paste of flour and tears, and I felt, as they say, a lot better, kind of lighthearted. For manly reasons I understood, but which made me feel no shame, Mr. County had been mortified by the outburst: he retired to the front of the shop.

Mrs. County poured coffee for herself and sat down. "I don't pretend to follow what's going on," she said. "The way I hear it, Miss Dolly broke up housekeeping because of some disagreement with Verena?" I wanted to say the situation was more complicated than that, but wondered, as I tried to array events, if really it was. "Now," she continued thoughtfully, "it may sound as though I'm talking against Dolly: I'm not. But this is what I feel—you people should go home, Dolly ought to make her peace with Verena: that's what she's always done, and you can't turn around at her time of life. Also, it sets a poor example for the town, two sisters quarreling, one of them sitting in a tree; and Judge Charlie Cool, for the first time in my life I feel sorry for those sons of his. Leading citizens have to behave themselves; otherwise the entire place goes to pieces. For instance, have you seen that wagon in the square? Well then, you better go have a look. Family of cowboys, they are. Evangelists, C.C. says—all I know is there's been a great racket over them and something to do with Dolly." Angrily she puffed up a paper sack. "I want you to tell her what I said: go home. And here, Collin, take along some cinnamon rolls. I know how Dolly dotes on them."

As I left the bakery the bells of the courthouse clock were ringing eight, which meant that it was seven-thirty. This clock has always run a half-hour fast. Once an expert was imported to repair it; at the end of almost a week's tinkering he recommended, as the only remedy, a stick of dynamite; the town council voted he be paid in full, for there was a general feeling of pride that the clock had proved so incorrigible. Around the square a few store-keepers were preparing to open; broom-sweepings fogged doorways, rolled trashbarrels berated the cool cat-quiet streets. At the Early Bird, a better grocery store than Verena's Jitney Jungle, two colored boys were fancying the window with cans of Hawaiian pineapple. On the south side of the square, beyond the cane benches where in all seasons sit the peaceful, perishing old men, I saw the wagon Mrs. County had spoken of—in reality an old truck contrived with tarpaulin covering to resemble the western wagons of history. It looked forlorn and foolish standing alone in the empty square. A homemade sign, perhaps four feet high, crested the cab like a shark's fin. Let Little Homer Honey Lasso Your Soul For The Lord. Painted on the other side there was a blistered greenish grinning head topped by a ten-gallon hat. I would not have thought it a portrait of anything human, but, according to a notice, this was: Child Wonder Little Homer Honey. With nothing more to see, for there was no one around the truck, I took myself toward the jail, which is a box-shaped brick building next door to the Ford Motor Company. I'd been inside it once. Big Eddie Stover had taken me there, along with a dozen other boys and men; he'd walked into the drugstore and said come over to the jail if you want to see something. The attraction was a thin handsome gipsy boy they'd taken off a freight train; Big Eddie gave him a quarter and told him to let down his pants; nobody could believe the size of it, and one of the men said, "Boy, how come they keep you locked up when you got a crowbar like that?" For weeks you could tell girls who had heard that joke: they giggled every time they passed the jail.

There is an unusual emblem decorating a side wall of the jail. I asked Dolly, and she said that in her youth she remembers it as a candy advertisement. If so, the lettering has vanished; what remains is a chalky tapestry: two flamingo-pink trumpeting angels swinging, swooping above a huge horn filled with fruit like a Christmas stocking; embroidered on the brick, it seems a faded mural, a faint tattoo, and sunshine flutters the imprisoned angels as though they were the spirits of thieves. I knew the risk I was taking, parading around in plain sight; but I walked past the jail, then back, and whistled, later whispered Catherine, Catherine, hoping this would bring her to the window. I realized which was her window: on the sill, reflecting beyond the bars, I saw a bowl of goldfish, the one thing, as subsequently we learned, she'd asked to have brought her. Orange flickerings of the fish fanned around the coral castle, and I thought of the morning I'd helped Dolly find it, the castle, the pearl pebbles. It had been the beginning and, chilled suddenly by a thought of what the end could be, Catherine coldly shadowed and peering downward, I prayed she would not come to the window: she would have seen no one, for I turned and ran.

Riley kept me waiting in the car more than two hours. By the time he showed up he was himself in such a temper I didn't dare show any of my own. It seems he'd gone home and found his sisters, Anne and Elizabeth, and Maude Riordan, who had spent the night, still lolling abed: not just that, but Coca-Cola bottles and cigarette butts all over the parlor. Maude took the blame: she confessed to having invited some boys over to listen to the radio and dance; but it was the sisters who got punished. He'd dragged them out of bed and whipped them. I asked what did he mean, whipped them? Turned them over my knee, he said, and whipped them with a tennis shoe. I couldn't picture this; it conflicted with my sense of Elizabeth's dignity. You're too hard on those girls, I said, adding vindictively: Maude, now there's the bad one. He took me seriously, said yes he'd intended to whip her if only because she'd called him the kind of names he wouldn't take off anybody; but before he could catch her she'd bolted out the back door. I thought to myself maybe at last Maude's had her bait of you.

Riley's ragged hair was glued down with brilliantine; he

smelled of lilac water and talcum. He didn't have to tell me he'd been to the barber's; or why.

Though he has since retired, there was in those days an exceptional fellow running the barbershop. Amos Legrand. Men like the Sheriff, for that matter Riley Henderson, oh everybody come to think of it, said: that old sis. But they didn't mean any harm; most people enjoyed Amos and really wished him well. A little monkeyman who had to stand on a box to cut your hair, he was agitated and chattery as a pair of castanets. All his steady customers he called honey, men and women alike, it made no difference to him. "Honey," he'd say, "it's about time you got this hair cut: was about to buy you a package of bobby-pins." Amos had one tremendous gift: he could tattle along on matters of true interest to businessmen and girls of ten—everything from what price Ben Jones got for his peanut crop to who would be invited to Mary Simpson's birthday party.

It was natural that Riley should have gone to him to get the news. Of course he repeated it straightforwardly; but I could imagine Amos, hear his hummingbird whirr: "There you are, honey, that's how it turns out when you leave money lying around. And of all people, Verena Talbo: here we thought she trotted to the bank with every dime came her way. Twelve thousand seven hundred dollars. But don't think it stops there. Seems Verena and this Dr. Ritz were going into business together, that's why she bought the old canning factory. Well get this: she gave Ritz over ten thousand to buy machinery, mercy knows what, and now it turns out he never bought one blessed penny's worth. Pocketed the whole thing. As for him, they've located not hide nor hair; South America, that's where they'll find him when and if. I never was somebody to insinuate any monkeyshines went on between him and her; I said Verena Talbo's too particular: honey, that Jew had the worst case of dandruff I've ever seen on a human head. But a smart woman like her, maybe she *was* stuck on him. Then all this to-do with her sister, the uproar over that. I don't wonder Doc Carter's giving her shots. But Charlie Cool's the one kills me: what do you make of him out there catching his death?"

We cleared town on two wheels; pop, pulp, insects spit against the windshield. The dry starched blue day whistled round us, there was not a cloud. And yet I swear storms foretell themselves in my bones. This is a nuisance common to old people, but fairly rare with anyone young. It's as though a damp rumble of thunder had sounded in your joints. The way I hurt, I felt nothing less than a hurricane could be headed our way, and said so to Riley, who said go on, you're crazy, look at the sky. We were making a bet about it when, rounding that bad curve so convenient to the cemetery, Riley winced and froze his brakes; we skidded long enough for a detailed review of our lives.

It was not Riley's fault: square in the road and struggling along like a lame cow was the Little Homer Honey wagon. With a clatter of collapsing machinery it came to a dead halt. In a moment the driver climbed out, a woman.

She was not young, but there was a merriness in the see-saw of her hips, and her breasts rubbed and nudged against her peach-colored blouse in such a coaxing way. She wore a fringed chamois skirt and knee-high cowboy boots, which was a mistake, for you felt that her legs, if fully exposed, would have been the best part. She leaned on the car door. Her eyelids drooped as though the lashes weighed intolerably; with the tip of her tongue she wettened her very red lips. "Good morning, fellows," she said, and it was a dragging slow-fuse voice. "I'd appreciate a few directions."

"What the hell's wrong with you?" said Riley, asserting himself. "You nearly made us turn over."

"I'm surprised you mention it," said the woman, amiably tossing her large head; her hair, an invented apricot color, was meticulously curled, and the curls, shaken out, were like bells with no music in them. "You were speeding, dear," she reproved him complacently. "I imagine there's a law against it; there are laws against everything, especially here."

Riley said, "There should be a law against that truck. A broken-down pile like that, it oughtn't to be allowed."

"I know, dear," the woman laughed. "Trade with you. Though I'm afraid we couldn't all fit into this car; we're even a bit squeezed in the wagon. Could you help me with a cigarette? That's a doll, thanks." As she lighted the cigarette I noticed how gaunt her hands were, rough; the nails were unpainted and one of them was black as though she'd crushed it in a door. "I was told that out this way we'd find a Miss Talbo. Dolly Talbo. She seems to be living in a tree. I wish you'd kindly show us where . . ."

Back of her there appeared to be an entire orphanage emptying out of the truck. Babies barely able to toddle on their rickety bowlegs, towheads dribbling ropes of snot, girls old enough to wear brassieres, and a ladder of boys, man-sized some of them. I counted up to ten, this including a set of crosseyed twins and a diapered baby being lugged by a child not more than five. Still, like a magician's rabbits, they kept coming, multiplied until the road was thickly populated.

"These all yours?" I said, really anxious; in another count I'd made a total of fifteen. One boy, he was about twelve and had tiny steel-rimmed glasses, flopped around in a ten-gallon hat like a walking mushroom. Most of them wore a few cowboy items, boots, at least a rodeo scarf. But they were a discouraged-looking lot, and sickly too, as though they'd lived years off boiled potatoes and onions. They pressed around the car, ghostly quiet except for the youngest who thumped the headlights and bounced on the fenders.

"Sure enough, dear: all mine," she answered, swatting at a mite of a girl playing maypole on her leg. "Sometimes I figure we've picked up one or two that don't belong," she added with a shrug, and several of the children smiled. They seemed to adore her. "Some of their daddies are dead; I guess the rest are living—one way and another: either case it's no concern of ours. I take it you weren't at our meeting last night. I'm Sister Ida, Little Homer Honey's mother." I wanted to know which one was Little Homer. She blinked around and singled out the spectacled boy who, wobbling up under his hat, saluted us: "Praise Jesus. Want a whistle?" and, swelling his cheeks, blasted a tin whistle.

"With one of those," explained his mother, tucking up her back hairs, "you can give the devil a scare. They have a number of practical uses as well."

"Two bits," the child bargained. He had a worried little face white as cold cream. The hat came down to his eyebrows.

I would have bought one if I'd had the money. You could see they were hungry. Riley felt the same, at any rate he produced fifty cents and took two of the whistles. "Bless you," said Little Homer, slipping the coin between his teeth and biting hard. "There's so much counterfeit going around these days," his mother confided apologetically. "In our branch of endeavor you wouldn't expect that kind of trouble," she said, sighing. "But if you kindly would show us—we can't go on much more, just haven't got the gas."

Riley told her she was wasting her time. "Nobody there any more," he said, racing the motor. Another driver, blockaded behind us, was honking his horn.

"Not in the tree?" Her voice was plaintive above the motor's

impatient roar. "But where will we find her then?" Her hands
were trying to hold back the car. "We've important business,
we . . ."

Riley jumped the car forward. Looking back, I saw them
watching after us in the raised and drifting road dust. I said
to Riley, and was sullen about it, that we ought to have found
out what they wanted.

And he said: "Maybe I know."

He did know a great deal, Amos Legrand having informed
him thoroughly on the subject of Sister Ida. Although she'd
not previously been to our town, Amos, who does a little
traveling now and then, claimed to have seen her once at a
fair in Bottle, which is a county town not far from here. Nor,
apparently, was she a stranger to the Reverend Buster who,
the instant she arrived, had hunted out the Sheriff and de-
manded an injunction to prevent the Little Homer Honey
troupe from holding any meetings. Racketeers, he called them;
and argued that the so-called Sister Ida was known throughout
six states as an infamous trollop: think of it, fifteen children
and no sign of a husband! Amos, too, was pretty sure she'd
never been married; but in his opinion a woman so industrious
was entitled to respect. The Sheriff said didn't he have enough
problems? and said: Maybe those fools have the right idea, sit
in a tree and mind your own business—for five cents he'd go
out there and join them. Old Buster told him in that case he
wasn't fit to be Sheriff and ought to hand in his badge. Meanwhile, Sister Ida had, without legal interference, called an evening of prayers and shenanigans under the oak trees in the
square. Revivalists are popular in this town; it's the music, the
chance to sing and congregate in the open air. Sister Ida and
her family made a particular hit; even Amos, usually so criti-
cal, told Riley he'd missed something: those kids really could
shout, and that Little Homer Honey, he was cute as a button
dancing and twirling a rope. Everybody had a grand time except the Reverend and Mrs. Buster, who had come to start a
fuss. What got their goat was when the children started haul-
ing in God's Washline, a rope with clothespins to which you
could attach a contribution. People who never dropped a dime
in Buster's collection plate were hanging up dollar bills. It was
more than he could stand. So he'd skipped off to the house on
Talbo Lane and had a small shrewd talk with Verena, whose
support, he realized, was necessary if he were going to get ac-
tion. According to Amos, he'd incited Verena by telling her

some hussy of a revivalist was describing Dolly as an infidel, an enemy of Jesus, and that Verena owed it to the Talbo name to see this woman was run out of town. It was unlikely that at the time Sister Ida had ever heard the name Talbo. But sick as she was, Verena went right to work; she rang up the Sheriff and said now look here Junius, I want these tramps run clear across the county line. Those were orders; and old Buster made it his duty to see they were carried out. He accompanied the Sheriff to the square where Sister Ida and her brood were cleaning up after the meeting. It had ended in a real scuffle, mainly because Buster, charging illegal gain, had insisted on confiscating the money gathered off God's Washline. He got it, too—along with a few scratches. It made no difference that many bystanders had taken Sister Ida's side: the Sheriff told them they'd better be out of town by noon the next day. Now after I'd heard all this I said to Riley why, when these people had been wrongly treated, hadn't he wanted to be more helpful? You'd never guess the answer he gave me. In dead earnest he said a loose woman like that was no one to associate with Dolly.

A twig fire fizzed under the tree; Riley collected leaves for it, while the Judge, his eyes smarting with smoke, set about the business of our midday meal. We were the indolent ones, Dolly and I. "I'm afraid," she said, dealing a game of Rook, "really afraid Verena's seen the last of that money. And you know, Collin, I doubt if it's losing the money that hurts her most. For whatever reason, she trusted him: Dr. Ritz, I mean. I keep remembering Maudie Laura Murphy. The girl who worked in the post office. She and Verena were very close. Lord, it was a great blow when Maudie Laura took up with that whiskey salesman, married him. I couldn't criticize her; 'twas only fitting if she loved the man. Just the same, Maudie Laura and Dr. Ritz, maybe those are the only two Verena ever trusted, and both of them—well, it could take the heart out of anyone." She thumbed the Rook cards with wandering attention. "You said something before—about Catherine."

"About her goldfish. I saw them in the window."

"But not Catherine?"

"No, the goldfish, that's all. Mrs. County was awfully nice: she said she was going to send some dinner around to the jail."

She broke one of Mrs. County's cinnamon rolls and picked out the raisins. "Collin, suppose we let them have their way,

gave up, that is: they'd have to let Catherine go, wouldn't
they?" Her eyes tilted toward the heights of the tree, searching, it seemed, a passage through the braided leaves. "Should
I—let myself lose?"

"Mrs. County thinks so: that we should go home."

"Did she say why?"

"Because—she did run on. Because you always have. Always made your peace, she said."

Dolly smiled, smoothed her long skirt; sifting rays placed
rings of sun upon her fingers. "Was there ever a choice? It's
what I want, a choice. To know I could've had another life,
all made of my own decisions. That would be making my
peace, and truly." She rested her eyes on the scene below,
Riley cracking twigs, the Judge hunched over a steaming pot.
"And the Judge, Charlie, if we gave up it would let him down
so badly. Yes," she tangled her fingers with mine, "he is very
dear to me," and an immeasurable pause lengthened the moment, my heart reeled, the tree closed inward like a folding
umbrella.

"This morning, while you were away, he asked me to marry
him."

As if he'd heard her, the Judge straightened up, a schoolboy
grin reviving the youthfulness of his countrified face. He
waved: and it was difficult to disregard the charm of Dolly's
expression as she waved back. It was as though a familiar
portrait had been cleaned and, turning to it, one discovered a
fleshy luster, clearer, till then unknown colors: whatever else,
she could never again be a shadow in the corner.

"And now—don't be unhappy, Collin," she said, scolding me,
I thought, for what she must have recognized as my resent-
ment.

"But are you . . .?"

"I've never earned the privilege of making up my own mind;
when I do, God willing, I'll know what is right. Who else,"
she said, putting me off further, "did you see in town?"

I would have invented someone, a story to retrieve her, for
she seemed to be moving forward into the future, while I,
unable to follow, was left with my sameness. But as I described Sister Ida, the wagon, the children, told the wherefores
of their run-in with the Sheriff and how we'd met them on the
road inquiring after the lady in the tree, we flowed together
again like a stream that for an instant an island had separated.
Though it would have been too bad if Riley had heard me be-
traying him, I went so far as to repeat what he'd said about a

woman of Sister Ida's sort not being fit company for Dolly.
She had a proper laugh over this; then, with sudden soberness:
"But it's wicked—taking the bread out of children's mouths
and using my name to do it. Shame on them!" She straightened her hat determinedly. "Collin, lift yourself; you and I are
going for a little walk. I'll bet those people are right where
you left them. Leastways, we'll see."

The Judge tried to prevent us, or at any rate maintained
that if Dolly wanted a stroll he would have to accompany us.
It went a long way toward mollifying my jealous rancor
when Dolly told him he'd best tend to his chores: with Collin
along she'd be safe enough—it was just to stretch our legs a bit.

As usual, Dolly could not be hurried. It was her habit, even
when it rained, to loiter along an ordinary path as though she
were dallying in a garden, her eyes primed for the sight of
precious medicine flavorings, a sprig of penny-royal, sweet-
mary and mint, useful herbs whose odor scented her clothes.
She saw everything first, and it was her one real vanity to
prefer that she, rather than you, point out certain discoveries:
a birdtrack bracelet, an eave of icicles—she was always calling
come see the cat-shaped cloud, the ship in the stars, the face
of frost. In this slow manner we crossed the grass, Dolly amas-
sing a pocketful of withered dandelions, a pheasant's quill: I
thought it would be sundown before we reached the road.

Fortunately we had not that far to go: entering the cemetery, we found Sister Ida and all her family encamped among
the graves. It was like a lugubrious playground. The crosseyed
twins were having their hair cut by older sisters, and Little
Homer was shining his boots with spit and leaves; a nearly
grown boy, sprawled with his back against a tombstone, picked
melancholy notes on a guitar. Sister Ida was suckling the baby;
it lay curled against her breasts like a pink ear. She did not
rise when she realized our presence, and Dolly said, "I do believe you're sitting on my father."

For a fact it was Mr. Talbo's grave, and Sister Ida, ad-
dressing the headstone (Uriah Fenwick Talbo, 1844-1922,
Good Soldier, Dear Husband, Loving Father) said, "Sorry,
soldier." Buttoning her blouse, which made the baby wail, she
started to her feet.

"Please don't; I only meant—to introduce myself."

Sister Ida shrugged, "He was beginning to hurt me anyway,"
and rubbed herself appropriately. "You again," she said, eyeing
me with amusement. "Where's your friend?"

"I understand . . ." Dolly stopped, disconcerted by the maze of children drawing in around her; "Did you," she went on, attempting to ignore a boy no bigger than a jackrabbit who, having raised her skirt, was sternly examining her shanks, "wish to see me? I'm Dolly Talbo."

Shifting the baby, Sister Ida threw an arm around Dolly's waist, embraced her, actually, and said, as though they were the oldest friends, "I knew I could count on you, Dolly. Kids," she lifted the baby like a baton, "tell Dolly we never said a word against her!"

The children shook their heads, mumbled, and Dolly seemed touched. "We can't leave town, I kept telling them," said Sister Ida, and launched into the tale of her predicament. I wished that I could have a picture of them together, Dolly, formal, as out of fashion as her old face-veil, and Sister Ida with her fruity lips, fun-loving figure. "It's a matter of cash; they took it all. I ought to have them arrested, that puke-faced Buster and what's-his-name, the Sheriff: thinks he's King Kong." She caught her breath; her cheeks were like a raspberry patch. "The plain truth is, we're stranded. Even if we'd ever heard of you, it's not our policy to speak ill of anyone. Oh I know that was just the excuse; but I figured you could straighten it out and . . ."

"I'm hardly the person—dear me," said Dolly.

"But what would you do? with a half gallon of gas, maybe not that, fifteen mouths and a dollar ten? We'd be better off in jail."

Then, "I have a friend," Dolly announced proudly, "a brilliant man, he'll know an answer," and I could tell by the pleased conviction of her voice that she believed this one hundred per cent. "Collin, you scoot ahead and let the Judge know to expect company for dinner."

Licketysplit across the field with the grass whipping my legs: couldn't wait to see the Judge's face. It was not a disappointment. "Lordylaw!" he said, raring back, rocking forward; "Sixteen people," and, observing the meager stew simmering on the fire, struck his head. For Riley's benefit I tried to make out it was none of my doing, Dolly's meeting Sister Ida; but he just stood there skinning me with his eyes: it could have led to bitter words if the Judge hadn't sent us scurrying. He fanned up his fire, Riley fetched more water, and into the stew we tossed sardines, hotdogs, green bay-leaves, in fact whatever lay at hand, including an entire box of Saltines which the Judge claimed would help thicken it: a few stuffs got mixed in by mistake—coffee grounds, for instance. Having reached that

overwrought hilarious state achieved by cooks at family re-
unions, we had the gall to stand back and congratulate ourselves: Riley gave me a forgiving, comradely punch, and as the
first of the children appeared the Judge scared them with the
vigor of his welcome.

None of them would advance until the whole herd had as-
sembled. Whereupon Dolly, apprehensive as a woman exhibit-
ing the results of an afternoon at an auction, brought them
forward to be introduced. The children made a rollcall of
their names: Beth, Laurel, Sam, Lillie, Ida, Cleo, Kate, Homer,
Harry—here the melody broke because one small girl refused
to give her name. She said it was a secret. Sister Ida agreed
that if she thought it a secret, then so it should remain.

"They're all so fretful," she said, favorably affecting the
Judge with her smoky voice and grasslike eyelashes. He pro-
longed their handshake and overdid his smile, which struck me
as peculiar conduct in a man who, not three hours before, had
asked a woman to marry him, and I hoped that if Dolly
noticed it would give her pause. But she was saying, "Why
certain they're fretful: hungry as they can be," and the Judge,
with a hearty clap and a boastful nod towards the stew, promised he'd fix that soon enough. In the meantime, he thought it
would be a good idea if the children went to the creek and
washed their hands. Sister Ida vowed they'd wash more than
that. They needed to, I'll tell you.

There was trouble with the little girl who wanted her name
a secret; she wouldn't go, not unless her papa rode her piggy-
back. "You are too my papa," she told Riley, who did not
contradict her. He lifted her onto his shoulders, and she was
tickled to death. All the way to the creek she acted the cut-up,
and when, with her hands thrust over his eyes, Riley stumbled
blindly into a bullis vine, she ripped the air with in-heaven
shrieks. He said he'd had enough of that and down you go.
"Please: I'll whisper you my name." Later on I remembered to
ask him what the name had been. It was Texaco Gasoline;
because those were such pretty words.

The creek is nowhere more than knee-deep; glossy beds of
moss green the banks, and in the spring snowy dew-drops and
dwarf violets flourish there like floral crumbs for the new bees
whose hives hang in the waterbays. Sister Ida chose a place
on the bank from which she could supervise the bathing. "No
cheating now—I want to see a lot of commotion." We did.
Suddenly girls old enough to be married were trotting around
and not a stitch on; boys, too, big and little all in there to-

gether naked as jaybirds. It was as well that Dolly had stayed
behind with the Judge; and I wished Riley had not come either,
for he was embarrassing in his embarrassment. Seriously,
though, it's only now, seeing the kind of man he turned out to
be, that I understand the paradox of his primness: he wanted
so to be respectable that the defections of others somehow
seemed to him backsliding on his own part.

Those famous landscapes of youth and woodland water—
in after years how often, trailing through the cold rooms of
museums, I stopped before such a picture, stood long haunted
moments having it recall that gone scene, not as it was, a band
of goose-fleshed children dabbling in an autumn creek, but as
the painting presented it, husky youths and wading water-
diamonded girls; and I've wondered then, wonder now, how
they fared, where they went in this world, that extraordinary
family.

"Beth, give your hair a douse. Stop splashing Laurel, I mean
you Buck, you quit that. All you kids get behind your ears,
mercy knows when you'll have the chance again." But presently Sister Ida relaxed and left the children at liberty. "On
such a day as this . . ." she sank against the moss; with the full
light of her eyes she looked at Riley, "There is something:
the mouth, the same jug ears—cigarette, dear?" she said, im-
pervious to his distaste for her. A smoothing expression suggested for a moment the girl she had been. "On such a day as
this . . .

". . . but in a sorrier place, no trees to speak of, a house in
a wheatfield and all alone like a scarecrow. I'm not complain-
ing: there was mama and papa and my sister Geraldine, and
we were sufficient, had plenty of pets and a piano and good
voices every one of us. Not that it was easy, what with all the
heavy work and only the one man to do it. Papa was a sickly
man besides. Hired hands were hard to come by, nobody
liked it way out there for long: one old fellow we thought a
heap of, but then he got drunk and tried to burn down the
house. Geraldine was going on sixteen, a year older than me,
and nice to look at, both of us were that, when she got it into
her head to marry a man who'd run the place with papa. But
where we were there wasn't much to choose from. Mama gave
us our schooling, what of it we had, and the closest town was
ten miles. That was the town of Youfry, called after a family;
the slogan was You Won't Fry In Youfry: because it was up
a mountain and well-to-do people went there in the summer.
So the summer I'm thinking of Geraldine got waitress work

at the Lookout Hotel in Youfry. I used to hitch a ride in on Saturdays and stay the night with her. This was the first either of us had ever been away from home. Geraldine didn't care about it particular, town life, but as for me I looked toward those Saturdays like each of them was Christmas and my birthday rolled into one. There was a dancing pavilion, it didn't cost a cent, the music was free and the colored lights. I'd help Geraldine with her work so we could go there all the sooner; we'd run hand in hand down the street, and I used to start dancing before I got my breath—never had to wait for a partner, there were five boys to every girl, and we were the prettiest girls anyway. I wasn't boy-crazy especially, it was the dancing—sometimes everyone would stand still to watch me waltz, and I never got more than a glimpse of my partners, they changed so fast. Boys would follow us to the hotel, then call under our window Come out! Come out! and sing, so silly they were—Geraldine almost lost her job. Well we'd lie awake considering the night in a practical way. She was not romantic, my sister; what concerned her was which of our beaux was surest to make things easier out home. It was Dan Rainey she decided on. He was older than the others, twenty-five, a man, not handsome in the face, he had jug ears and freckles and not much chin, but Dan Rainey, oh he was smart in his own steady way and strong enough to lift a keg of nails. End of summer he came out home and helped bring in the wheat. Papa liked him from the first, and though mama said Geraldine was too young, she didn't make any ruckus about it. I cried at the wedding, and thought it was because the nights at the dancing pavilion were over, and because Geraldine and I would never lie cozy in the same bed again. But as soon as Dan Rainey took over everything seemed to go right; he brought out the best in the land and maybe the best in us. Except when winter came on, and we'd be sitting round the fire, sometimes the heat, something made me feel just faint. I'd go stand in the yard with only my dress on, it was like I couldn't feel the cold because I'd become a piece of it, and I'd close my eyes, waltz round and round, and one night, I didn't hear him sneaking up, Dan Rainey caught me in his arms and danced me for a joke. Only it wasn't such a joke. He had feelings for me; way back in my head I'd known it from the start. But he didn't say it, and I never asked him to; and it wouldn't have come to anything provided Geraldine hadn't lost her baby. That was in the spring. She was mortally afraid of snakes, Geraldine, and it was seeing one that did it; she was collecting eggs, it was only a chicken snake, but it scared her so bad she dropped her baby four months too soon. I don't know what happened to her—got cross and mean, got where she'd fly out about anything. Dan Rainey took the worst of it; he kept out of her way as much as he could; used to roll himself in a blanket and sleep down in the wheatfield. I knew if I stayed there—so I went to Youfry and got Geraldine's old job at the hotel. The dancing pavilion, it was the same as the summer before, and I was even prettier: one boy nearly killed another over who was going to buy me an orangeade. I can't say I didn't enjoy myself, but my mind wasn't on it; at the hotel they asked where was my mind—always filling the sugar bowl with salt, giving people spoons to cut their meat. I never went home the whole summer. When the time came—it was such a day as this, a fall day blue as eternity—I didn't let them know I was coming, just got out of the coach and walked three miles through the wheat stacks till I found Dan Rainey. He didn't speak a word, only plopped down and cried like a baby. I was that sorry for him, and loved him more than tongue can tell."

Her cigarette had gone out. She seemed to have lost track of the story; or worse, thought better of finishing it. I wanted to stamp and whistle, the way rowdies do at the picture-show when the screen goes unexpectedly blank; and Riley, though less bald about it, was impatient too. He struck a match for her cigarette: starting at the sound, she remembered her voice again, but it was as if, in the interval, she'd traveled far ahead.

"So papa swore he'd shoot him. A hundred times Geraldine said tell us who it was and Dan here'll take a gun after him. I laughed till I cried; sometimes the other way round. I said well I had no idea; there were five or six boys in Youfry could be the one, and how was I to know? Mama slapped my face when I said that. But they believed it; even after a while I think Dan Rainey believed it—wanted to anyway, poor unhappy fellow. All those months not stirring out of the house; and in the middle of it papa died. They wouldn't let me go to the funeral, they were so ashamed for anyone to see. It happened this day, with them off at the burial and me alone in the house and a sandy wind blowing rough as an elephant, that I got in touch with God. I didn't by any means deserve to be Chosen: up till then, mama'd had to coax me to learn my Bible verses; afterwards, I memorized over a thousand in less than three months. Well I was practicing a tune on the piano, and suddenly a window broke, the whole room turned topsy-turvy, then fell together again, and someone was with me, papa's spirit I thought; but the wind died down peaceful as spring—He was there, and standing as He made me, straight, I opened my arms to welcome Him. That was twenty-six years ago last February the third; I was sixteen, I'm forty-two now, and I've never wavered. When I had my baby I didn't call Geraldine or Dan Rainey or anybody, only lay there whispering my verses one after the other and not a soul knew Danny was born till they heard him holler. It was Geraldine named him that. He was hers, everyone thought so, and people round the countryside rode over to see her new baby, brought presents, some of them, and the men hit Dan Rainey on the back and told him what a fine son he had. Soon as I was able I moved thirty miles away to Stoneville, that's a town double the size of Youfry and where they have a big mining camp. Another girl and I, we started a laundry, and did a good business on account of in a mining town there's mostly bachelors. About twice a month I went home to see Danny; I was seven years going back and forth; it was the only pleasure I had, and a strange one, considering how it tore me up every time: such a beautiful boy, there's no describing. But Geraldine died for me to touch him: if I kissed him she'd come near to jumping out of her skin; Dan Rainey wasn't much different, he was so scared I wouldn't leave well enough alone. The last time I ever was home I asked him would he meet me in Youfry. Because for a crazy long while I'd had an idea, which was: if I could live it again, if I could bear a child that would be a twin to Danny. But I was wrong to think it could have the same father. It would've been a dead child, born dead: I looked at Dan Rainey (it was the coldest day, we sat by the empty dancing pavilion, I remember he never took his hands out of his pockets) and sent him away without saying why it was I'd asked him to come. Then years spent hunting the likeness of him. One of the miners in Stoneville, he had the same freckles, yellow eyes; a goodhearted boy, he obliged me with Sam, my oldest. As best I recall, Beth's father was a dead ringer for Dan Rainey; but being a girl, Beth didn't favor Danny. I forget to tell you that I'd sold my share of the laundry and gone to Texas—had restaurant work in Amarillo and Dallas. But it wasn't until I met Mr. Honey that I saw why the Lord had chosen me and what my task was to be. Mr. Honey possessed the True Word; after I heard him preach that first time I went round to see him: we hadn't talked twenty minutes than he said I'm going to marry you provided you're not married a'ready. I said no I'm not married, but I've got some family; fact is, there was five by then. Didn't faze him a bit. We got married a week later on Valentine's Day. He wasn't a young man, and he didn't look a particle like Dan Rainey; stripped of his boots he couldn't make it to my shoulder; but when the Lord brought us together He knew certain what He was doing: we had Roy, then Pearl and Kate and Cleo and Little Homer —most of them born in that wagon you saw up there. We traveled all over the country carrying His Word to folks who'd never heard it before, not the way my man could tell it. Now I must mention a sad circumstance, which is: I lost Mr. Honey. One morning, this was in a queer part of Louisiana, Cajun parts, he walked off down the road to buy some groceries: you know we never saw him again. He disappeared right into thin air. I don't give a hoot what the police say; he wasn't the kind to run out on his family; no sir it was foul play."

"Or amnesia," I said. "You forget everything, even your own name."

"A man with the whole Bible on the tip of his tongue— would you say he was liable to forget something like his name? One of them Cajuns murdered him for his amethyst ring. Naturally I've known men since then; but not love. Lillie Ida, Laurel, the other kids, they happened like. Seems somehow I can't get on without another life kicking under my heart: feel so sluggish otherwise."

When the children were dressed, some with their clothes inside out, we returned to the tree where the older girls, bending over the fire, dried and combed their hair. In our absence Dolly had cared for the baby; she seemed now not to want to give it back: "I wish one of us had had a baby, my sister or Catherine," and Sister Ida said yes, it was entertaining and a satisfaction too. We sat finally in a circle around the fire. The stew was too hot to taste, which perhaps accounted for its thorough success, and the Judge, who had to serve it in rotation, for there were only three cups, was full of gay stunts and nonsense that exhilarated the children: Texaco Gasoline decided she'd made a mistake—the Judge, not Riley, was her papa, and the Judge rewarded her with a trip to the moon, swung her, that is, high over his head: *Some flocked south, Some flocked west, You go flying after the rest, Away! Awhee!* Sister Ida said say you're pretty strong. Of course he lapped it up, all but asked her to feel his muscles. Every quarter-minute he peeked to see if Dolly were admiring him. She was.

The croonings of a ringdove wavered among the long last lances of sunlight. Chill green, blues filtered through the air as though a rainbow had dissolved around us. Dolly shivered: "There's a storm nearby. I've had the notion all day." I looked at Riley triumphantly: hadn't I told him?

"And it's getting late," said Sister Ida. "Buck, Homer—you boys chase up to the wagon. Gracious knows who's come along and helped themselves. Not," she added, watching her sons vanish on the darkening path, "that there's a whole lot to take, nothing much except my sewing machine. So, Dolly? Have you ..."

"We've discussed it," said Dolly turning to the Judge for confirmation.

"You'd win your case in court, no question of it," he said, very professional. "For once the law would be on the right side. As matters stand, however ..."

Dolly said, "As matters stand," and pressed into Sister Ida's hand the forty-seven dollars which constituted our cash asset; in addition, she gave her the Judge's big gold watch. Contemplating these gifts, Sister Ida shook her head as though she should refuse them. "It's wrong. But I thank you."

A light thunder rolled through the woods, and in the perilous quiet of its wake Buck and Little Homer burst upon the path like charging cavalry. "They're coming! They're coming!" both got out at once, and Little Homer, pushing back his hat, gasped: "We ran all the way."

"Make sense, boy: who?"

Little Homer swallowed. "Those fellows. The Sheriff one, and I don't know how many more. Coming down through the grass. With guns, too."

Thunder rumbled again; tricks of wind rustled our fire.

"All right now," said the Judge, assuming command. "Everybody keep their heads." It was as though he'd planned for this moment, and he rose to it, I do concede, gloriously. "The women, you little kids, get up in the treehouse. Riley, see that the rest of you scatter out, shinny up those other trees and take a load of rocks." When we'd followed these directions, he alone remained on the ground; firm-jawed, he stayed there guarding the tense twilighted silence like a captain who will not abandon his drowning ship.

Six

Five of us roosted in the sycamore tree that overhung the path. Little Homer was there, and his brother Buck, a scowling boy with rocks in either hand. Across the way, straddling the limbs of a second sycamore, we could see Riley surrounded by the older girls: in the deepening burnished light their white faces glimmered like candle-lanterns. I thought I felt a raindrop: it was a bead of sweat slipping along my cheek; still, and though the thunder lulled, a smell of rain intensified the odor of leaves and woodsmoke. The overloaded tree-house gave an evil creak; from my vantage point, its tenants seemed a single creature, a many-legged, many-eyed spider upon whose head Dolly's hat sat perched like a velvet crown.

In our tree everybody pulled out the kind of tin whistles Riley had bought from Little Homer: good to give the devil a scare, Sister Ida had said. Then Little Homer took off his huge hat and, removing from its vast interior what was perhaps God's Washline, a thick long rope, at any rate, proceeded to make a sliding noose. As he tested its efficiency, stretched and tightened the knot, his steely miniature spectacles cast such a menacing sparkle that, edging away, I put the distance of another branch between us. The Judge, patrolling below, hissed to stop moving around up there; it was his last order before the invasion began.

The invaders themselves made no pretense at stealth. Swinging their rifles against the undergrowth like canecutters, they swaggered up the path, nine, twelve, twenty strong. First, Junius Candle, his Sheriff's star winking in the dusk; and after him, Big Eddie Stover, whose squint-eyed search of our hiding places reminded me of those newspaper picture puzzles; find five boys and an owl in this drawing of a tree. It requires someone cleverer than Big Eddie Stover. He looked straight at me, and through me. Not many of that gang would have troubled you with their braininess: good for nothing but a lick of salt and swallow of beer most of them. Except I recognized Mr. Hand, the principal at school, a decent enough fellow taken all around, no one, you would have thought, to involve himself in such shabby company on so shameful an errand. Curiosity explained the attendance of Amos Legrand; he was there, and silent for once: no wonder: as though he were a walking-stick, Verena was leaning a hand on his head, which came not quite to her hip. A grim Reverend Buster ceremoniously supported her other arm. When I saw Verena I felt a numbed reliving of the terror I'd known when, after my mother's death, she'd come to our house to claim me. Despite what seemed a lameness, she moved with her customary tall authority and, accompanied by her escorts, stopped under our sycamore.

The Judge didn't give an inch; toe to toe with the Sheriff, he stood his ground as if there were a drawn line he dared the other to cross.

It was at this crucial moment that I noticed Little Homer. He gradually was lowering his lasso. It crawled, dangled like a snake, the wide noose open as a pair of jaws, then fell, with an expert snap, around the neck of the Reverend Buster, whose strangling outcry Little Homer stifled by giving the rope a mighty tug.

His friends hadn't long to consider old Buster's predicament, his blood-gorged face and flailing arms; for Little Homer's success inspired an all-out attack: rocks flew, whistles shrilled like the shriekings of savage birds, and the men, pummeling each other in the general rout, took refuge where they could, principally under the bodies of comrades already fallen. Verena had to box Amos Legrand's ears: he tried to sneak up under her skirt. She alone, you might say, behaved like a real man: shook her fists at the trees and cursed us blue.

At the height of the din, a shot slammed like an iron door. It quelled us all, the serious endless echo of it; but in the hush that followed we heard a weight come crashing through the opposite sycamore.

It was Riley, falling; and falling: slowly, relaxed as a killed cat. Covering their eyes, the girls screamed as he struck a branch and splintered it, hovered, like the torn leaves, then in a bleeding heap hit the ground. No one moved toward him.

Until at last the Judge said, "Boy, my boy," and in a trance sank to his knees; he caressed Riley's limp hands. "Have mercy. Have mercy, son: answer." Other men, sheepish and frightened, closed round; some offered advice which the Judge seemed unable to comprehend. One by one we dropped down from the trees, and the children's gathering whisper is he dead? is he dead? was like the moan, the delicate roar of a sea-trumpet. Doffing their hats respectfully, the men made an aisle for Dolly; she was too stunned to take account of them, or of Verena, whom she passed without seeing.

"I want to know," said Verena, in tones that summoned attention, ". . . which of you fools fired that gun?"

The men guardedly looked each other over: too many of them fixed on Big Eddie Stover. His jowls trembled, he licked his lips: "Hell, I never meant to shoot nobody; was doing my duty, that's all."

"Not all," Verena severely replied. "I hold you responsible, Mr. Stover."

At this Dolly turned round; her eyes, vague beyond the veiling, seemed to frame Verena in a gaze that excluded everyone else. "Responsible? No one is that; except ourselves."

Sister Ida had replaced the Judge at Riley's side; she completely stripped off his shirt. "Thank your stars, it's his shoulder," she said, and the relieved sighs, Big Eddie's alone, would have floated a kite. "He's fairly knocked out, though. Some of you fellows better get him to a doctor." She stopped Riley's bleeding with a bandage torn off his shirt. The Sheriff and three of his men locked arms, making a litter on which to carry him. He was not the only one who had to be carried; the Reverend Buster had also come to considerable grief: loose-limbed as a puppet, and too weak to know the noose still hung around his neck, he needed several assistants to get up the path. Little Homer chased after him: "Hey, hand me back my rope!"

Amos Legrand waited to accompany Verena; she told him to go without her as she had no intention of leaving unless

Dolly—hesitating, she looked at the rest of us, Sister Ida in particular: "I would like to speak with my sister alone."

With a wave of her hand that quite dismissed Verena, Sister Ida said, "Never mind, lady. We're on our way." She hugged Dolly. "Bless us, we love you. Don't we, kids?" Little Homer said, "Come with us, Dolly. We'll have such good times. I'll give you my sparkle belt." And Texaco Gasoline threw herself upon the Judge, pleading for him to go with them, too. Nobody seemed to want me.

"I'll always remember that you asked me," said Dolly, her eyes hurrying as though to memorize the children's faces. "Good luck. Good-bye. Run now," she raised her voice above new and nearer thunder, "run, it's raining."

It was a tickling feathery rain fine as a gauze curtain, and as they faded into the folds of it, Sister Ida and her family, Verena said: "Do I understand you've been conniving with that—woman? After she made a mockery of our name?"

"I don't think you can accuse me of conniving with anyone," Dolly answered serenely. "Especially not with bullies who," she a little lost control, "steal from children and drag old women into jail. I can't set much store by a name that endorses such methods. It ought to be a mockery."

Verena received this without flinching. "You're not yourself," she said, as if it were a clinical opinion.

"You'd best look again: I am myself." Dolly seemed to pose for inspection. She was as tall as Verena, as assured; nothing about her was incomplete or blurred. "I've taken your advice: stopped hanging my head, I mean. You told me it made you dizzy. And not many days ago," she continued, "you told me that you were ashamed of me. Of Catherine. So much of our lives had been lived for you; it was painful to realize the waste that had been. Can you know what it is, such a feeling of waste?"

Scarcely audible, Verena said, "I do know," and it was as if her eyes crossed, peered inward upon a stony vista. It was the expression I'd seen when, spying from the attic, I'd watched her late at night brooding over the Kodak pictures of Maudie Laura Murphy, Maudie Laura's husband and children. She swayed, she put a hand on my shoulder; except for that, I think she might have fallen.

"I imagined I would go to my dying day with the hurt of it. I won't. But it's no satisfaction, Verena, to say that I'm ashamed of you, too."

It was night now; frogs, sawing insects celebrated the slow-falling rain. We dimmed as though the wetness had snuffed the light of our faces. Verena sagged against me. "I'm not well," she said in a skeleton voice. "I'm a sick woman, I am, Dolly."

Somewhat unconvinced, Dolly approached Verena, presently touched her, as though her fingers could sense the truth. "Collin," she said, "Judge, please help me with her into the tree." Verena protested that she couldn't go climbing trees; but once she got used to the idea she went up easily enough. The raftlike tree-house seemed to be floating over shrouded vaporish waters; it was dry there, however, for the mild rain had not penetrated the parasol of leaves. We drifted in a current of silence until Verena said, "I have something to say, Dolly. I could say it more easily if we were alone."

The Judge crossed his arms. "I'm afraid you'll have to put up with me, Miss Verena." He was emphatic, though not belligerent. "I have an interest in the outcome of what you might have to say."

"I doubt that: how so?" she said, recovering to a degree her exalted manner.

He lighted a stub of candle, and our sudden shadows stooped over us like four eavesdroppers. "I don't like talking in the dark," he said. There was a purpose in the proud erectness of his posture: it was, I thought, to let Verena know she was dealing with a man, a fact too few men in her experience had enough believed to assert. She found it unforgivable. "You don't remember, do you, Charlie Cool? Fifty years ago, more maybe. Some of you boys came blackberry stealing out at our place. My father caught your cousin Seth, and I caught you. It was quite a licking you got that day."

The Judge did remember; he blushed, smiled, said: "You didn't fight fair, Verena."

"I fought fair," she told him drily. "But you're right—since neither of us like it, let's not talk in the dark. Frankly, Charlie, you're not a welcome sight to me. My sister couldn't have gone through such tommyrot if you hadn't been goading her on. So I'll thank you to leave us; it can be no further affair of yours."

"But it is," said Dolly. "Because Judge Cool, Charlie . . ." she dwindled, appeared for the first time to question her boldness.

"Dolly means that I have asked her to marry me."

"That," Verena managed after some suspenseful seconds, "is," she said, regarding her gloved hands, "remarkable. Very. I wouldn't have credited either of you with so much imagination. Or is it that I am imagining? Quite likely I'm dreaming of myself in a wet tree on a thundery night. Except I never have dreams, or perhaps I only forget them. This one I suggest we all forget."

"I'll own up: I think it is a dream, Miss Verena. But a man who doesn't dream is like a man who doesn't sweat: he stores up a lot of poison."

She ignored him; her attention was with Dolly, Dolly's with her: they might have been alone together, two persons at far ends of a bleak room, mutes communicating in an eccentric sign-language, subtle shifting of the eye; and it was as though, then, Dolly gave an answer, one that sapped all color from Verena's face. "I see. You've accepted him, have you?"

The rain had thickened, fish could have swum through the air; like a deepening scale of piano notes, it struck its blackest chord, and drummed into a downpour that, though it threat- ened, did not at once reach us: drippings leaked through the leaves, but the tree-house stayed a dry seed in a soaking plant. The Judge put a protective hand over the candle; he waited as anxiously as Verena for Dolly's reply. My impatience equaled theirs, yet I felt exiled from the scene, again a spy peering from the attic, and my sympathies, curiously, were nowhere; or rather, everywhere: a tenderness for all three ran together like raindrops, I could not separate them, they expanded into a human oneness.

Dolly, too. She could not separate the Judge from Verena. At last, excruciatingly, "I can't," she cried, implying failures beyond calculation. "I said I would know what was right. But it hasn't happened; I don't know: do other people? A choice, I thought: to have had a life made of my own decisions . . ."

"But we have had our lives," said Verena. "Yours has been nothing to despise, I don't think you've required more than you've had; I've envied you always. Come home, Dolly. Leave decisions to me: that, you see, has been my life."

"Is it true, Charlie?" Dolly asked, as a child might ask where do falling stars fall? and: "Have we had our lives?"

"We're not dead," he told her; but it was as if, to the ques- tioning child, he'd said stars fall into space: an irrefutable, still unsatisfactory answer. Dolly could not accept it: "You don't have to be dead. At home, in the kitchen, there is a geranium that blooms over and over. Some plants, though, they bloom just the once, if at all, and nothing more happens to them. They live, but they've had their life."

"Not you," he said, and brought his face nearer hers, as

though he meant their lips to touch, yet wavered, not daring it. Rain had tunneled through the branches, it fell full weight; rivulets of it streamed off Dolly's hat, the veiling clung to her cheeks; with a flutter the candle failed. "Not me."

Successive strokes of lightning throbbed like veins of fire, and Verena, illuminated in that sustained glare, was not anyone I knew; but some woman woebegone, wasted—with eyes once more drawn toward each other, their stare settled on an inner territory, a withered country; as the lightning lessened, as the hum of rain sealed us in its multiple sounds, she spoke, and her voice came so weakly from so very far, not expecting, it seemed, to be heard at all. "Envied you, Dolly. Your pink room. I've only knocked at the doors of such rooms, not often —enough to know that now there is no one but you to let me in. Because little Morris, little Morris—help me, I loved him, I did. Not in a womanly way; it was, oh I admit it, that we were kindred spirits. We looked each other in the eye, we saw the same devil, we weren't afraid; it was—merry. But he outsmarted me; I'd known he could, and hoped he wouldn't, and he did, and now: it's too long to be alone, a lifetime. I walk through the house, nothing is mine: your pink room, your kitchen, the house is yours, and Catherine's too, I think. Only don't leave me, let me live with you. I'm feeling old, I want my sister."

The rain, adding its voice to Verena's, was between them, Dolly and the Judge, a transparent wall through which he could watch her losing substance, recede before him as earlier she had seemed to recede before me. More than that, it was as if the tree-house were dissolving. Lunging wind cast overboard the soggy wreckage of our Rook cards, our wrapping papers; animal crackers crumbled, the rain-filled mason jars spilled over like fountains; and Catherine's beautiful scrapquilt was ruined, a puddle. It was going: like the doomed houses rivers in flood float away; and it was as though the Judge were trapped there—waving to us as we, the survivors, stood ashore. For Dolly had said, "Forgive me; I want my sister, too," and the Judge could not reach her, not with his arms, not with his heart: Verena's claim was too final.

Somewhere near midnight the rain slackened, halted; wind barreled about wringing out the trees. Singly, like delayed guests arriving at a dance, appearing stars pierced the sky. It was time to leave. We took nothing with us: left the quilt to rot, spoons to rust; and the tree-house, the woods we left to winter.

Seven

For quite a while it was Catherine's custom to date events as
having occurred before or after her incarceration. "Prior," she
would begin, "to the time That One made a jailbird of me."
As for the rest of us, we could have divided history along
similar lines; that is, in terms of before and after the tree-
house. Those few autumn days were a monument and a sign-
post.

Except to collect his belongings, the Judge never again en-
tered the house he'd shared with his sons and their wives, a
circumstance that must have suited them, at least they made
no protest when he took a room at Miss Bell's boarding house.
This was a brown solemn establishment which lately has been
turned into a funeral home by an undertaker who saw that to
effect the correct atmosphere a minimum of renovation would
be necessary. I disliked going past it, for Miss Bell's guests,
ladies thorny as the blighted rosebushes littering the yard, occupied the porch in a dawn-to-dark marathon of vigilance.
One of them, the twice-widowed Mamie Canfield, specialized
in spotting pregnancies (some legendary fellow is supposed to
have told his wife Why waste money on a doctor? just trot
yourself past Miss Bell's: Mamie Canfield, she'll let the world
know soon enough whether you is or ain't). Until the Judge
moved there, Amos Legrand was the only man in residence
at Miss Bell's. He was a godsend to the other tenants: the
moments most sacred to them were when, after supper, Amos
swung in the seat-swing with his little legs not touching the

floor and his tongue trilling like an alarm-clock. They vied
with each other in knitting him socks and sweaters, tending to
his diet: at table all the best things were saved for his plate—
Miss Bell had trouble keeping a cook because the ladies were
forever poking around in the kitchen wanting to make a deli-
cacy that would tempt their pet. Probably they would have
done the same for the Judge, but he had no use for them,
never, so they complained, stopped to pass the time of day.

The last drenching night in the tree-house had left me with
a bad cold, Verena with a worse one; and we had a sneezing
nurse, Dolly. Catherine wouldn't help: "Dollyheart, you can
do like you please—tote That One's slopjar till you drop in
your tracks. Only don't count on me to lift a finger. I've put
down the load."

Rising at all hours of the night, Dolly brought the syrups
that eased our throats, stoked the fires that kept us warm.
Verena did not, as in other days, accept such attention simply
as her due. "In the spring," she promised Dolly, "we'll make a
trip together. We might go to the Grand Canyon and call on
Maudie Laura. Or Florida: you've never seen the ocean." But
Dolly was where she wanted to be, she had no wish to travel:
"I wouldn't enjoy it, seeing the things I've known shamed by
nobler sights."

Doctor Carter called regularly to see us, and one morning
Dolly asked would he mind taking her temperature; she felt
so flushed and weak in the legs. He put her straight to bed,
and she thought it was very humorous when he told her she
had walking pneumonia. "Walking pneumonia," she said to the
Judge, who had come to visit her, "it must be something new,
I've never heard of it. But I do feel as though I were sky-
larking along on a pair of stilts. Lovely," she said and fell
asleep.

For three, nearly four days she never really woke up. Catherine stayed with her, dozing upright in a wicker chair and
growling low whenever Verena or I tiptoed into the room.
She persisted in fanning Dolly with a picture of Jesus, as though
it were summertime; and it was a disgrace how she ignored
Doctor Carter's instructions: "I wouldn't feed that to a hog,"
she'd declare, pointing to some medicine he'd sent around.
Finally Doctor Carter said he wouldn't be responsible unless
the patient were removed to a hospital. The nearest hospital
was in Brewton, sixty miles away. Verena sent over there for
an ambulance. She could have saved herself the expense, because Catherine locked Dolly's door from the inside and said

the first one to rattle the knob would need an ambulance themselves. Dolly did not know where they wanted to take her;
wherever it was, she begged not to go: "Don't wake me," she
said, "I don't want to see the ocean."

Toward the end of the week she could sit up in bed; a few
days later she was strong enough to resume correspondence
with her dropsy-cure customers. She was worried by the unfilled orders that had piled up; but Catherine, who took the
credit for Dolly's improvement, said, "Shoot, it's no time we'll
be out there boiling a brew."

Every afternoon, promptly at four, the Judge presented himself at the garden gate and whistled for me to let him in;
by using the garden gate, rather than the front door, he lessened the chance of encountering Verena—not that she objected to his coming: indeed, she wisely supplied for his visits a
bottle of sherry and a box of cigars. Usually he brought Dolly
a gift, cakes from the Katydid Bakery or flowers, bronze balloonlike chrysanthemums which Catherine swiftly confiscated
on the theory that they ate up all the nourishment in the air.
Catherine never learned he had proposed to Dolly; still, intuiting a situation not quite to her liking, she sharply chaperoned the Judge's visits and, while swigging at the sherry that
had been put out for him, did most of the talking as well. But
I suspect that neither he nor Dolly had much to say of a
private nature; they accepted each other without excitement,
as people do who are settled in their affections. If in other
ways he was a disappointed man, it was not because of Dolly,
for I believe she became what he'd wanted, the one person in
the world—to whom, as he'd described it, everything can be
said. But when everything can be said perhaps there is nothing
more to say. He sat beside her bed, content to be there and
not expecting to be entertained. Often, drowsy with fever, she
went to sleep, and if, while she slept, she whimpered or
frowned, he wakened her, welcoming her back with a daylight
smile.

In the past Verena had not allowed us to have a radio;
cheap melodies, she contended, disordered the mind; moreover, there was the expense to consider. It was Doctor Carter
who persuaded her that Dolly should have a radio; he thought
it would help reconcile her to what he foresaw as a long
convalescence. Verena bought one, and paid a good price, I
don't doubt; but it was an ugly hood-shaped box crudely varnished. I took it out in the yard and painted it pink. Even so
Dolly wasn't certain she wanted it in her room; later on, you

couldn't have pried it away from her. That radio was always
hot enough to hatch a chicken, she and Catherine played it so
much. They favored broadcasts of football games. "Please
don't," Dolly admonished the Judge when he attempted to
explain the rules of this game. "I like a mystery. Everybody
shouting, having such a fine time: it might not sound so large
and happy if I knew why." Primarily the Judge was peeved
because he couldn't get Dolly to root for any one team. She
thought both sides should win: "They're all nice boys, I'm sure."

Because of the radio Catherine and I had words one afternoon. It was the afternoon Maude Riordan was playing in a
broadcast of the state musical competition. Naturally I wanted
to hear her, Catherine knew that, but she was tuned in on a
Tulane-Georgia Tech game and wouldn't let me near the radio.
I said, "What's come over you, Catherine? Selfish, dissatisfied,
always got to have your own way, why you're worse than
Verena ever was." It was as though, in lieu of prestige lost
through her encounter with the law, she'd had to double her
power in the Talbo house: we at least would have to respect
her Indian blood, accept her tyranny. Dolly was willing; in the
matter of Maude Riordan, however, she sided with me: "Let
Collin find his station. It wouldn't be Christian not to listen to
Maude. She's a friend of ours."

Everyone who heard Maude agreed that she should've won
first prize. She placed second, which pleased her family, for it
meant a half-scholarship in music at the University. Still it
wasn't fair, because she performed beautifully, much better
than the boy who won the larger prize. She played her father's
serenade, and it seemed to me as pretty as it had that day in
the woods. Since that day I'd wasted hours scribbling her
name, describing in my head her charms, her hair the color
of vanilla ice cream. The Judge arrived in time to hear the
broadcast, and I know Dolly was glad because it was as if
we were reunited again in the leaves with music like butterflies flying.

Some days afterwards I met Elizabeth Henderson on the
street. She'd been at the beauty parlor, for her hair was finger-
waved, her nails tinted, she did look grown-up and I com-
plimented her. "It's for the party. I hope your costume is
ready." Then I remembered: the Halloween party to which
she and Maude had asked me to contribute my services as a
fortuneteller. "You can't have forgotten? Oh, Collin," she said,
"we've worked like dogs! Mrs. Riordan is making a *wine*
punch. I shouldn't be surprised if there's drunkenness and

everything. And after all it's a celebration for Maude, because she won the prize, and because," Elizabeth glanced along the street, a glum perspective of silent houses and telephone poles, "she'll be going away—to the University, you know." A loneliness fell around us, we did not want to go our separate ways: I offered to walk her home.

On our way we stopped by the Katydid where Elizabeth placed an order for a Halloween cake, and Mrs. C. C. County, her apron glittering with sugar crystals, appeared from the oven room to inquire after Dolly's condition. "Doing well as can be expected I suppose," she lamented. "Imagine it, walking pneumonia. My sister, now she had the ordinary lying-down kind. Well, we can be thankful Dolly's in her own bed; it eases my mind to know you people are home again. Ha ha, guess we can laugh about all that foolishness now. Look here, I've just pulled out a pan of doughnuts; you take them to Dolly with my blessings." Elizabeth and I ate most of those doughnuts before we reached her house. She invited me in to have a glass of milk and finish them off.

Today there is a filling station where the Henderson house used to be. It was some fifteen draughty rooms casually nailed together, a place stray animals would have claimed if Riley had not been a gifted carpenter. He had an outdoor shed, a combination of workshop and sanctuary, where he spent his mornings sawing lumber, shaving shingles. Its wall-shelves sagged with the relics of outgrown hobbies: snakes, bees, spiders preserved in alcohol, a bat decaying in a bottle; ship models. A boyhood enthusiasm for taxidermy had resulted in a pitiful zoo of nasty-odored beasts: an eyeless rabbit with maggot-green fur and ears that drooped like a bloodhound's —objects better off buried. I'd been lately to see Riley several times; Big Eddie Stover's bullet had shattered his shoulder, and the curse of it was he had to wear an itching plaster cast which weighed, he said, a hundred pounds. Since he couldn't drive his car, or hammer a proper nail, there wasn't much for him to do except loaf around and brood.

"If you want to see Riley," said Elizabeth, "you'll find him out in the shed. I expect Maude's with him."

"Maude Riordan?" I had reason to be surprised, because on the occasions I'd visited Riley he'd made a point of our sitting in the shed; the girls wouldn't bother us there, for it was, he'd boasted, one threshold no female was permitted to cross.

"Reading to him. Poetry, plays. Maude's been absolutely adorable. And it's not as though my brother had ever treated

her with common human decency. But she's let bygones be bygones. I guess coming so near to being killed the way he was,
I guess that would change a person—make them more recep-
tive to the finer things. He lets her read to him by the hour."

The shed, shaded by fig trees, was in the back yard. Ma-
tronly Plymouth hens waddled about its doorstep picking at
the seeds of last summer's fallen sunflowers. On the door a
childhood word in faded whitewash feebly warned Beware!
It aroused a shyness in me. Beyond the door I could hear
Maude's voice—her poetry voice, a swooning chant certain
louts in school had dearly loved to mimic. Anyone who'd been
told Riley Henderson had come to this, they'd have said that
fall from the sycamore had affected his head. Stealing over to
the shed's window, I got a look at him: he was absorbed in
sorting the insides of a clock and, to judge from his face,
might have been listening to nothing more uplifting than the
hum of a fly; he jiggled a finger in his ear, as though to re-
lieve an irritation. Then, at the moment I'd decided to startle
them by rapping on the window, he put aside his clockworks
and, coming round behind Maude, reached down and shut the
book from which she was reading. With a grin he gathered in
his hand twists of her hair—she rose like a kitten lifted by the
nape of its neck. It was as though they were edged with light,
some brilliance that smarted my eyes. You could see it wasn't
the first time they'd kissed.

Not one week before, because of his experience in such
matters, I'd taken Riley into my confidence, confessed to him
my feelings for Maude: please look. I wished I were a giant so
that I could grab hold of that shed and shake it to a splinter;
knock down the door and denounce them both. Yet—of what
could I accuse Maude? Regardless of how bad she'd talked
about him I'd always known she was heartset on Riley. It
wasn't as if there had ever been an understanding between the
two of us; at the most we'd been good friends: for the last
few years, not even that. As I walked back through the yard
the pompous Plymouth hens cackled after me tauntingly.

Elizabeth said, "You didn't stay long. Or weren't they there?"

I told her it hadn't seemed right to interrupt. "They were
getting on so well with the finer things."

But sarcasm never touched Elizabeth: she was, despite the
subtleties her soulful appearance promised, too literal a person. "Wonderful, isn't it?"

"Wonderful."

"Collin—for heaven's sake: what are you sniveling about?"

"Nothing. I mean, I've got a cold."

"Well I hope it doesn't keep you away from the party. Only you must have a costume. Riley's coming as the devil."

"That's appropriate."

"Of course we want you in a skeleton suit. I know there's only a day left. . . ."

I had no intention of going to the party. As soon as I got home I sat down to write Riley a letter. Dear Riley . . . Dear Henderson. I crossed out the dear; plain Henderson would do. Henderson, your treachery has not gone unobserved. Pages were filled with recording the origins of our friendship, its honorable history; and gradually a feeling grew that there must be a mistake: such a splendid friend would not have wronged me. Until, toward the end, I found myself deliriously telling him he was my best friend, my brother. So I threw these ravings in a fireplace and five minutes later was in Dolly's room asking what were the chances of my having a skeleton suit made by the following night.

Dolly was not much of a seamstress, she had her difficulties lifting a hemline. This was also true of Catherine; it was in Catherine's makeup, however, to pretend professional status in all fields, particularly those in which she was least competent. She sent me to Verena's drygoods store for seven yards of their choicest black satin. "With seven yards there ought to be some bits left over: me and Dolly can trim our petticoats." Then she made a show of tape-measuring my lengths and widths, which was sound procedure except that she had no idea of how to apply such information to scissors and cloth. "This little piece," she said, hacking off a yard, "it'd make somebody lovely bloomers. And this here," snip, snip, ". . . . a black satin collar would dress up my old print considerable." You couldn't have covered a midget's shame with the amount of material allotted me.

"Catherine, now dear, we mustn't think of our own needs," Dolly warned her.

They worked without recess through the afternoon. The Judge, during his usual visit, was forced to thread needles, a job Catherine despised: "Makes my flesh crawl, like stuffing worms on a fishhook." At suppertime she called quits and went home to her house among the butterbean stalks.

But a desire to finish had seized Dolly; and a talkative exhilaration. Her needle soared in and out of the satin; like the seams it made, her sentences linked in a wiggling line. "Do you think," she said, "that Verena would let me give a party? Now that I have so many friends? There's Riley, there's Charlie, couldn't we ask Mrs. County, Maude and Elizabeth? In the spring; a garden party—with a few fireworks. My father was a great hand for sewing. A pity I didn't inherit it from him. So many men sewed in the old days; there was one friend of Papa's that won I don't know how many prizes for his scrap-quilts. Papa said it relaxed him after the heavy rough work around a farm. Collin. Will you promise me something? I was against your coming here, I've never believed it was right, raising a boy in a houseful of women. Old women and their prejudices. But it was done; and somehow I'm not worried about it now: you'll make your mark, you'll get on. It's this that I want you to promise me: don't be unkind to Catherine, try not to grow too far away from her. Some nights it keeps me wide awake to think of her forsaken. There," she held up my suit, "let's see if it fits."

It pinched in the crotch and in the rear drooped like an old man's B.V.D.'s; the legs were wide as sailor pants, one sleeve stopped above my wrist, the other shot past my finger-tips. It wasn't, as Dolly admitted, very stylish. "But when we've painted on the bones . . ." she said. "Silver paint. Verena bought some once to dress up a flagpole—before she took against the government. It should be somewhere in the attic, that little can. Look under the bed and see if you can locate my slippers."

She was forbidden to get up, not even Catherine would permit that. "It won't be any fun if you scold," she said and found the slippers herself. The courthouse clock had chimed eleven, which meant it was ten-thirty, a dark hour in a town where respectable doors are locked at nine; it seemed later still because in the next room Verena had closed her ledgers and gone to bed. We took an oil lamp from the linen closet and by its tottering light tiptoed up the ladder into the attic. It was cold up there; we set the lamp on a barrel and lingered near it as though it were a hearth. Sawdust heads that once had helped sell St. Louis hats watched while we searched; wherever we put our hands it caused a huffy scuttling of fragile feet. Overturned, a carton of mothballs clattered on the floor. "Oh, dear, oh, dear," cried Dolly, giggling, "if Verena hears that she'll call the Sheriff."

We unearthed numberless brushes; the paint, discovered beneath a welter of dried holiday wreaths, proved not to be silver but gold. "Of course that's better, isn't it? Gold, like a king's ransom. Only do see what else I've found." It was a shoebox secured with twine. "My valuables," she said, opening it under the lamp. A hollowed honeycomb was demonstrated against the light, a hornet's nest and a clove-stuck orange that age had robbed of its aroma. She showed me a blue perfect jaybird's egg cradled in cotton.

"I was too principled. So Catherine stole the egg for me, it was her Christmas present." She smiled; to me her face seemed a moth suspended beside the lamp's chimney, as daring, as destructible. "Charlie said that love is a chain of love. I hope you listened and understood him. Because when you can love one thing," she held the blue egg as preciously as the Judge had held a leaf, "you can love another, and that is owning, that is something to live with. You can forgive everything. Well," she sighed, "we're not getting you painted. I want to amaze Catherine; we'll tell her that while we slept the little people finished your suit. She'll have a fit."

Again the courthouse clock was floating its message, each note like a banner stirring above the chilled and sleeping town. "I know it tickles," she said, drawing a branch of ribs across my chest, "but I'll make a mess if you don't hold still." She dipped the brush and skated it along the sleeves, the trousers, designing golden bones for my arms and legs. "You must remember all the compliments: there should be many," she said as she immodestly observed her work. "Oh dear, oh dear . . ." She hugged herself, her laughter rollicked in the rafters. "Don't you see . . ."

For I was not unlike the man who painted himself into a corner. Freshly gilded front and back, I was trapped inside the suit: a fine fix for which I blamed her with a pointing finger.

"You have to whirl," she teased. "Whirling will dry you." She blissfully extended her arms and turned in slow ungainly circles across the shadows of the attic floor, her plain kimono billowing and her thin feet wobbling in their slippers. It was as though she had collided with another dancer: she stumbled, a hand on her forehead, a hand on her heart.

Far on the horizon of sound a train whistle howled, and it wakened me to the bewilderment puckering her eyes, the contractions shaking her face. With my arms around her, and the paint bleeding its pattern against her, I called Verena; somebody help me!

Dolly whispered, "Hush now, hush."

Houses at night announce catastrophe by their sudden pitiable radiance. Catherine dragged from room to room switching on lights unused for years. Shivering inside my wrecked

costume I sat in the glare of the entrance hall sharing a bench
with the Judge. He had come at once, wearing only a raincoat
slung over a flannel nightshirt. Whenever Verena approached
he brought his naked legs together primly, like a young girl.
Neighbors, summoned by our bright windows, came softly inquiring. Verena spoke to them on the porch: her sister, Miss
Dolly, she'd suffered a stroke. Doctor Carter would allow
none of us in her room, and we accepted this, even Catherine
who, when she'd set ablaze the last light, stood leaning her
head against Dolly's door.

There was in the hall a hat-tree with many antlers and a
mirror. Dolly's velvet hat hung there, and at sunrise, as breezes
trickled through the house, the mirror reflected its quivering
veil.

Then I knew as good as anything that Dolly had left us.
Some moments past she'd gone by unseen; and in my imagination I followed her. She had crossed the square, had come
to the church, now she'd reached the hill. The Indian grass
gleamed below her, she had that far to go.

It was a journey I made with Judge Cool the next September. During the intervening months we had not often en-
countered each other—once we met on the square and he
said to come see him any time I felt like it. I meant to, yet
whenever I passed Miss Bell's boarding house I looked the
other way.

I've read that past and future are a spiral, one coil con-
taining the next and predicting its theme. Perhaps this is so;
but my own life has seemed to me more a series of closed
circles, rings that do not evolve with the freedom of a spiral:
for me to get from one to the other has meant a leap, not a
glide. What weakens me is the lull between, the wait before I
know where to jump. After Dolly died I was a long while
dangling.

My own idea was to have a good time.

I hung around Phil's Café winning free beers on the pin-
ball machine; it was illegal to serve me beer, but Phil had it
on his mind that someday I would inherit Verena's money
and maybe set him up in the hotel business. I slicked my hair
with brilliantine and chased off to dances in other towns,
shined flashlights and threw pebbles at girls' windows late at
night. I knew a Negro in the country who sold a brand of
gin called Yellow Devil. I courted anyone who owned a car.

Because I didn't want to spend a waking moment in the

Talbo house. It was too thick with air that didn't move. Some stranger occupied the kitchen, a pigeon-toed colored girl who sang all day, the wavery singing of a child bolstering its spirit in an ominous place. She was a sorry cook. She let the kitchen's geranium plant perish. I had approved of Verena hiring her. I thought it would bring Catherine back to work.

On the contrary, Catherine showed no interest in routing the new girl. For she'd retired to her house in the vegetable garden. She had taken the radio with her and was very comfortable. "I've put down the load, and it's down to stay. I'm after my leisure," she said. Leisure fattened her, her feet swelled, she had to cut slits in her shoes. She developed exaggerated versions of Dolly's habits, such as a craving for sweet foods; she had her suppers delivered from the drugstore, two quarts of ice cream. Candy wrappers rustled in her lap. Until she became too gross, she contrived to squeeze herself into clothes that had belonged to Dolly; it was as though, in this way, she kept her friend with her.

Our visits together were an ordeal, and I made them grudgingly, resenting it that she depended on me for company. I let a day slip by without seeing her, then three, a whole week once. When I returned after an absence I imagined the silences in which we sat, her offhand manner, were meant reproachfully; I was too conscience-ridden to realize the truth, which was that she didn't care whether or not I came. One afternoon she proved it. Simply, she removed the cotton wads that jacked up her jaws. Without the cotton her speech was as unintelligible to me as it ordinarily was to others. It happened while I was making an excuse to shorten my call. She lifted the lid of a pot-bellied stove and spit the cotton into the fire; and her cheeks caved in, she looked starved. I think now this was not a vengeful gesture: it was intended to let me know that I was under no obligation: the future was something she preferred not to share.

Occasionally Riley rode me around—but I couldn't count on him or his car; neither were much available since he'd become a man of affairs. He had a team of tractors clearing ninety acres of land he'd bought on the outskirts of town; he planned to build houses there. Several locally important persons were impressed by another scheme of his: he thought the town should put up a silkmill in which every citizen would be a stockholder; aside from the possible profits, having an industry would increase our population. There was an enthusiastic editorial in the paper about this proposal; it went on

to say that the town should be proud of having produced a
man of young Henderson's enterprise. He grew a mustache;
he rented an office and his sister Elizabeth worked as his sec-
retary. Maude Riordan was installed at the State University,
and almost every week-end he drove his sisters over there; it
was supposed to be because the girls were so lonesome for
Maude. The engagement of Miss Maude Riordan to Mr. Riley
Henderson was announced in the *Courier* on April Fool's Day.

They were married the middle of June in a double-ring
ceremony. I acted as an usher, and the Judge was Riley's best
man. Except for the Henderson sisters, all the bridesmaids
were society girls Maude had known at the University; the
Courier called them beautiful debutantes, a chivalrous description. The bride carried a bouquet of jasmine and lilac; the
groom wore spats and stroked his mustache. They received a
sumptuous table-load of gifts. I gave them six cakes of scented
soap and an ashtray.

After the wedding I walked home with Verena under the
shade of her black umbrella. It was a blistering day, heatwaves
jiggled like a sound-graph of the celebrating Baptist bells, and
the rest of summer, a vista rigid as the noon street, lengthened before me. Summer, another autumn, winter again: not
a spiral, but a circle confined as the umbrella's shadow. If I
ever were to make the leap—with a heartskip, I made it.
"Verena, I want to go away."

We were at the garden gate; "I know. I do myself," she
said, closing her umbrella. "I'd hoped to make a trip with
Dolly. I wanted to show her the ocean." Verena had seemed
a tall woman because of her authoritative carriage; now she
stooped slightly, her head nodded. I wondered that I ever
could have been so afraid of her, for she'd grown feminine,
fearful, she spoke of prowlers, she burdened the doors with
bolts and spiked the roof with lightning rods. It had been her
custom the first of every month to stalk around collecting in
person the various rents owed her; when she stopped doing
this it caused an uneasiness in the town, people felt wrong
without their rainy day. The women said she's got no family,
she's lost without her sister; their husbands blamed Dr. Morris
Ritz: he knocked the gumption out of her, they said; and,
much as they had quarreled with Verena, held it against him.
Three years ago, when I returned to this town, my first task
was to sort the papers of the Talbo estate, and among Verena's
private possessions, her keys, her pictures of Maudie Laura
Murphy, I found a postcard. It was dated two months after

Dolly died, at Christmas, and it was from Paraguay: *As we say down here, Feliz Navidad. Do you miss me? Morris*. And I thought, reading it, of how her eyes had come permanently to have an uneven cast, an inward and agonized gaze, and I remembered how her eyes, watering in the brassy sunshine of Riley's wedding day, had straightened with momentary hope: "It could be a long trip. I've considered selling a few—a few properties. We might take a boat; you've never seen the ocean." I picked a sprig of honeysuckle from the vine flowering on the garden fence, and she watched me shred it as if I were pulling apart her vision, the voyage she saw for us. "Oh," she brushed at the mole that spotted her cheek like a tear, "well," she said in a practical voice, "what are your ambitions?"

So it was not until September that I called upon the Judge, and then it was to tell him good-bye. The suitcases were packed, Amos Legrand had cut my hair ("Honey, don't you come back here baldheaded. What I mean is, they'll try to scalp you up there, cheat you every way they can."); I had a new suit and new shoes, gray fedora ("Aren't you the cat's pajamas, Mr. Collin Fenwick?" Mrs. County exclaimed. "A lawyer you're going to be? And already dressed like one. No, child, I won't kiss you. I'd be mortified to dirty your finery with my bakery mess. You write us, hear?"): that very evening a train would rock me northward, parade me through the land to a city where in my honor pennants flurried.

At Miss Bell's they told me the Judge had gone out. I found him on the square, and it gave me a twinge to see him, a spruce sturdy figure with a Cherokee rose sprouting in his buttonhole, encamped among the old men who talk and spit and wait. He took my arm and led me away from them; and while he amiably advised me of his own days as a law student, we strolled past the church and out along the River Woods road. This road or this tree: I closed my eyes to fix their image, for I did not believe I would return, did not foresee that I would travel the road and dream the tree until they had drawn me back.

It was as though neither of us had known where we were headed. Quietly astonished, we surveyed the view from the cemetery hill, and arm in arm descended to the summer-burned, September-burnished field. A waterfall of color flowed across the dry and strumming leaves; and I wanted then for the Judge to hear what Dolly had told me: that it was a grass harp, gathering, telling, a harp of voices remembering a story. We listened.

MUSIC FOR CHAMELEONS

In these gems of reportage, Truman Capote takes true stories and real people and renders them with stylistic brio. Whether he was writing about an enigmatic killer who sends his victims macabre announcements of their forthcoming demise or swapping sexual gossip with a luminous Marilyn Monroe, Capote was an unparalleled observer of the social fauna of his time.

Nonfiction/Literature/0-679-74566-1

ANSWERED PRAYERS
The Unfinished Novel

Although Truman Capote's last novel was left unfinished when he died, its surviving chapters offer a devastating portrait of the high society and low life of his time. As it follows the picaresque career of P. B. Jones, a writer/gigolo of uncertain parentage and omnivorous erotic tastes, *Answered Prayers* careens from literary salons to high-priced whorehouse, displaying Capote at his most observant and murderously witty.

Fiction/Literature/0-679-75182-3

Available at your local bookstore, or call toll-free to order:
1-800-793-2665 (credit cards only).

VINTAGE INTERNATIONAL

____ The Ark Sakura by Kobo Abe	$12.00	0-679-72161-4
____ The Woman in the Dunes by Kobo Abe	$11.00	0-679-73378-7
____ Generations of Winter by Vassily Aksyonov	$13.00	0-679-76182-9
____ Chromos by Felipe Alfau	$11.00	0-679-73443-0
____ Locos: A Comedy of Gestures by Felipe Alfau	$8.95	0-679-72846-5
____ Dead Babies by Martin Amis	$11.00	0-679-73449-X
____ Einstein's Monsters by Martin Amis	$10.00	0-679-72996-8
____ London Fields by Martin Amis	$13.00	0-679-73034-6
____ Other People by Martin Amis	$10.00	0-679-73589-5
____ The Rachel Papers by Martin Amis	$11.00	0-679-73458-9
____ Success by Martin Amis	$10.00	0-679-73448-1
____ Time's Arrow by Martin Amis	$11.00	0-679-73572-0
____ Visiting Mrs. Nabokov and Other Excursions by Martin Amis	$12.00	0-679-75793-7
____ For Every Sin by Aharon Appelfeld	$9.95	0-679-72758-2
____ One Day of Life by Manlio Argueta	$10.00	0-679-73243-8
____ Obabakoak by Bernardo Atxaga	$12.00	0-679-74958-6
____ Collected Poems by W. H. Auden	$22.50	0-679-73197-0
____ The Dyer's Hand by W. H. Auden	$15.00	0-679-72484-2
____ Forewords and Afterwords by W. H. Auden	$15.00	0-679-72485-0
____ Selected Poems by W. H. Auden	$12.00	0-679-72483-4
____ Another Country by James Baldwin	$12.00	0-679-74471-1
____ Blues for Mister Charlie by James Baldwin	$10.00	0-679-76178-0
____ The Fire Next Time by James Baldwin	$8.00	0-679-74472-X
____ Going to Meet the Man by James Baldwin	$11.00	0-679-76179-9
____ Nobody Knows My Name by James Baldwin	$10.00	0-679-74473-8
____ Doctor Copernicus by John Banville	$10.00	0-679-73799-5
____ Ghosts by John Banville	$11.00	0-679-75512-8
____ Kepler by John Banville	$10.00	0-679-74370-7
____ Before She Met Me by Julian Barnes	$11.00	0-679-73609-3
____ Flaubert's Parrot by Julian Barnes	$10.00	0-679-73136-9
____ A History of the World in 10½ Chapters by Julian Barnes	$12.00	0-679-73137-7
____ Letters from London by Julian Barnes	$12.00	0-679-76161-6
____ Metroland by Julian Barnes	$10.00	0-679-73608-5
____ The Porcupine by Julian Barnes	$9.00	0-679-74482-7
____ Staring at the Sun by Julian Barnes	$10.00	0-679-74820-2
____ Talking It Over by Julian Barnes	$11.00	0-679-73687-5
____ The Italics Are Mine by Nina Berberova	$16.00	0-679-74537-8
____ The Tattered Cloak and Other Novels by Nina Berberova	$11.00	0-679-73366-3
____ About Looking by John Berger	$11.00	0-679-73655-7
____ And Our Faces, My Heart, Brief as Photos by John Berger	$10.00	0-679-73656-5
____ Another Way of Telling by John Berger and Jean Mohr	$17.00	0-679-73724-3
____ Corker's Freedom by John Berger	$11.00	0-679-75513-6
____ G. by John Berger	$13.00	0-679-73654-9
____ Keeping a Rendezvous by John Berger	$13.00	0-679-73714-6
____ Lilac and Flag by John Berger	$12.00	0-679-73719-7
____ Once in Europa by John Berger	$11.00	0-679-73716-2
____ Pig Earth by John Berger	$11.00	0-679-73715-4
____ The Sense of Sight by John Berger	$12.00	0-679-73722-7
____ The Success and Failure of Picasso by John Berger	$12.00	0-679-73725-1
____ Gathering Evidence by Thomas Bernhard	$14.00	0-679-73809-6
____ The Loser by Thomas Bernhard	$10.00	0-679-74179-8
____ A Man for All Seasons by Robert Bolt	$8.00	0-679-72822-8

VINTAGE INTERNATIONAL

___ The Sheltering Sky by Paul Bowles	$12.00	0-679-72979-8
___ An Act of Terror by André Brink	$14.00	0-679-74429-0
___ The Death of Virgil by Hermann Broch	$16.00	0-679-75548-9
___ Angels & Insects by A.S. Byatt	$12.00	0-679-75134-3
___ The Game by A.S. Byatt	$10.00	0-679-74256-5
___ Passions of the Mind by A.S. Byatt	$12.00	0-679-73678-6
___ Possession by A.S. Byatt	$12.00	0-679-73590-9
___ Sugar and Other Stories by A.S. Byatt	$10.00	0-679-74227-1
___ The Virgin in the Garden by A.S. Byatt	$12.00	0-679-73829-0
___ The Marriage of Cadmus and Harmony by Roberto Calasso	$13.00	0-679-73348-5
___ The Road to San Giovanni by Italo Calvino	$10.00	0-679-74348-0
___ Six Memos for the Next Millennium by Italo Calvino	$10.00	0-679-74237-9
___ Exile and the Kingdom by Albert Camus	$10.00	0-679-73385-X
___ The Fall by Albert Camus	$9.00	0-679-72022-7
___ The Myth of Sisyphus and Other Essays by Albert Camus	$9.00	0-679-73373-6
___ The Plague by Albert Camus	$10.00	0-679-72021-9
___ The Rebel by Albert Camus	$11.00	0-679-73384-1
___ The Stranger by Albert Camus	$8.00	0-679-72020-0
___ Answered Prayers by Truman Capote	$10.00	0-679-75182-3
___ Breakfast at Tiffany's by Truman Capote	$10.00	0-679-74565-3
___ The Grass Harp by Truman Capote	$10.00	0-679-74557-2
___ In Cold Blood by Truman Capote	$12.00	0-679-74558-0
___ Music for Chameleons by Truman Capote	$11.00	0-679-74566-1
___ Other Voices, Other Rooms by Truman Capote	$11.00	0-679-74564-5
___ The Fat Man in History by Peter Carey	$10.00	0-679-74332-4
___ The Tax Inspector by Peter Carey	$11.00	0-679-73598-4
___ Bullet Park by John Cheever	$11.00	0-679-73787-1
___ Falconer by John Cheever	$11.00	0-679-73786-3
___ Oh What a Paradise It Seems by John Cheever	$9.00	0-679-73785-5
___ The Wapshot Chronicle by John Cheever	$11.00	0-679-73899-1
___ The Wapshot Scandal by John Cheever	$11.00	0-679-73900-9
___ Age of Iron by J.M. Coetzee	$10.00	0-679-73292-6
___ After Henry by Joan Didion	$12.00	0-679-74539-4
___ A Book of Common Prayer by Joan Didion	$12.00	0-679-75486-5
___ Democracy by Joan Didion	$12.00	0-679-75485-7
___ Run River by Joan Didion	$11.00	0-679-75250-1
___ Salvador by Joan Didion	$9.00	0-679-75183-1
___ Anecdotes of Destiny and Ehrengard by Isak Dinesen	$12.00	0-679-74333-2
___ Last Tales by Isak Dinesen	$13.00	0-679-73640-9
___ Out of Africa and Shadows on the Grass by Isak Dinesen	$12.00	0-679-72475-3
___ Seven Gothic Tales by Isak Dinesen	$13.00	0-679-73641-7
___ Winter's Tales by Isak Dinesen	$12.00	0-679-74334-0
___ The Book of Daniel by E.L. Doctorow	$12.00	0-679-73657-3
___ Loon Lake by E.L. Doctorow	$11.00	0-679-73625-5
___ Ragtime by E.L. Doctorow	$12.00	0-679-73626-3
___ Welcome to Hard Times by E.L. Doctorow	$10.00	0-679-73627-1
___ World's Fair by E.L. Doctorow	$12.00	0-679-73628-X
___ Love, Pain, and the Whole Damn Thing by Doris Dörrie	$9.00	0-679-72992-5
___ Once Were Warriors by Alan Duff	$10.00	0-679-76181-0
___ The Assignment by Friedrich Dürrenmatt	$7.95	0-679-72233-5
___ Going to the Territory by Ralph Ellison	$13.00	0-679-76001-6
___ Invisible Man by Ralph Ellison	$11.00	0-679-72313-7

VINTAGE INTERNATIONAL

———— Shadow and Act by Ralph Ellison $13.00   0-679-76000-8

———— Scandal by Shusaku Endo $10.00   0-679-72355-2

———— Absalom, Absalom! by William Faulkner $11.00   0-679-73218-7

———— As I Lay Dying by William Faulkner $9.00   0-679-73225-X

———— Big Woods by William Faulkner $9.00   0-679-75252-8

———— Go Down, Moses by William Faulkner $10.00   0-679-73217-9

———— The Hamlet by William Faulkner $10.00   0-679-73653-0

———— Intruder in the Dust by William Faulkner $9.00   0-679-73651-4

———— Light in August by William Faulkner $10.00   0-679-73226-8

———— The Reivers by William Faulkner $10.00   0-679-74192-5

———— Sanctuary by William Faulkner $10.00   0-679-74814-8

———— The Sound and the Fury by William Faulkner $9.00   0-679-73224-1

———— The Unvanquished by William Faulkner $9.00   0-679-73652-2

———— The Good Soldier by Ford Madox Ford $10.00   0-679-72218-1

———— Howards End by E. M. Forster $10.00   0-679-72255-6

———— The Longest Journey by E. M. Forster $11.00   0-679-74815-6

———— A Room With a View by E. M. Forster $9.00   0-679-72476-1

———— Where Angels Fear to Tread by E. M. Forster $9.00   0-679-73634-4

———— Separation by Dan Franck $11.00   0-679-75444-X

———— Christopher Unborn by Carlos Fuentes $16.00   0-679-73222-5

———— The Story of My Wife by Milán Füst $8.95   0-679-72217-3

———— The Story of a Shipwrecked Sailor $9.00   0-679-72205-X
     by Gabriel García Márquez

———— The Tin Drum by Günter Grass $15.00   0-679-72575-X

———— Claudius the God by Robert Graves $14.00   0-679-72573-3

———— I, Claudius by Robert Graves $13.00   0-679-72477-X

———— Dispatches by Michael Herr $11.00   0-679-73525-9

———— Walter Winchell by Michael Herr $9.00   0-679-73393-0

———— The Swimming-Pool Library by Alan Hollinghurst $12.00   0-679-72256-4

———— I Served the King of England $12.00   0-679-72786-8
     by Bohumil Hrabal

———— An Artist of the Floating World by Kazuo Ishiguro $10.00   0-679-72266-1

———— A Pale View of Hills by Kazuo Ishiguro $10.00   0-679-72267-X

———— The Remains of the Day by Kazuo Ishiguro $11.00   0-679-73172-5

———— A Neil Jordan Reader by Neil Jordan $12.00   0-679-74834-2

———— Dubliners by James Joyce $10.00   0-679-73990-4

———— A Portrait of the Artist as a Young Man $9.00   0-679-73989-0
     by James Joyce

———— Ulysses by James Joyce $16.00   0-679-72276-9

———— The Devil's Own Work by Alan Judd $9.00   0-679-74745-1

———— The Emperor by Ryszard Kapuściński $9.00   0-679-72203-3

———— Shah of Shahs by Ryszard Kapuściński $10.00   0-679-73801-0

———— The Soccer War by Ryszard Kapuściński $11.00   0-679-73805-3

———— China Men by Maxine Hong Kingston $10.00   0-679-72328-5

———— Tripmaster Monkey by Maxine Hong Kingston $12.00   0-679-72789-2

———— The Woman Warrior by Maxine Hong Kingston $10.00   0-679-72188-6

———— Judge on Trial by Ivan Klíma $14.00   0-679-73756-1

———— Love and Garbage by Ivan Klíma $11.00   0-679-73755-3

———— Barabbas by Pär Lagerkvist $8.00   0-679-72544-X

———— The Plumed Serpent by D. H. Lawrence $12.00   0-679-73493-7

———— The Virgin & the Gipsy by D. H. Lawrence $10.00   0-679-74077-5

———— The Radiance of the King by Camara Laye $12.00   0-679-72200-9

———— Canopus in Argos by Doris Lessing $22.00   0-679-74184-4

———— The Fifth Child by Doris Lessing $9.00   0-679-72182-7

———— The Drowned and the Saved by Primo Levi $10.00   0-679-72186-X

———— My Traitor's Heart by Rian Malan $12.00   0-679-73215-2

VINTAGE INTERNATIONAL

____ The Great World by David Malouf	$12.00	0-679-74836-9
____ Remembering Babylon by David Malouf	$10.00	0-679-74951-9
____ Man's Fate by André Malraux	$12.00	0-679-72574-1
____ Buddenbrooks by Thomas Mann	$15.00	0-679-75260-9
____ Confessions of Felix Krull by Thomas Mann	$13.00	0-679-73904-1
____ Death in Venice and Seven Other Stories by Thomas Mann	$10.00	0-679-72206-8
____ Doctor Faustus by Thomas Mann	$14.00	0-679-73905-X
____ The Magic Mountain by Thomas Mann	$15.00	0-679-73645-X
____ Monopolies of Loss by Adam Mars-Jones	$11.00	0-679-74415-0
____ The Waters of Thirst by Adam Mars-Jones	$11.00	0-679-75960-3
____ Ancestors by William Maxwell	$12.00	0-679-75929-8
____ All the Pretty Horses by Cormac McCarthy	$12.00	0-679-74439-8
____ Blood Meridian by Cormac McCarthy	$11.00	0-679-72875-9
____ Child of God by Cormac McCarthy	$10.00	0-679-72874-0
____ The Crossing by Cormac McCarthy	$13.00	0-679-76084-9
____ The Orchard Keeper by Cormac McCarthy	$11.00	0-679-72872-4
____ Outer Dark by Cormac McCarthy	$10.00	0-679-72873-2
____ Suttree by Cormac McCarthy	$12.00	0-679-73632-8
____ The Cement Garden by Ian McEwan	$10.00	0-679-75018-5
____ The Comfort of Strangers by Ian McEwan	$9.00	0-679-74984-5
____ First Love, Last Rites by Ian McEwan	$10.00	0-679-75019-3
____ In Between the Sheets by Ian McEwan	$10.00	0-679-74983-7
____ The Collected Stories by John McGahern	$12.00	0-679-74401-0
____ Karma Cola by Gita Mehta	$10.00	0-679-75433-4
____ A River Sutra by Gita Mehta	$11.00	0-679-75247-1
____ The Captive Mind by Czeslaw Milosz	$11.00	0-679-72856-2
____ The Decay of the Angel by Yukio Mishima	$13.00	0-679-72243-2
____ Runaway Horses by Yukio Mishima	$13.00	0-679-72240-8
____ The Sailor Who Fell From Grace With the Sea by Yukio Mishima	$10.00	0-679-75015-0
____ The Sound of Waves by Yukio Mishima	$10.00	0-679-75268-4
____ Spring Snow by Yukio Mishima	$12.00	0-679-72241-6
____ The Temple of Dawn by Yukio Mishima	$14.00	0-679-72242-4
____ The Temple of the Golden Pavilion by Yukio Mishima	$11.00	0-679-75270-6
____ Such a Long Journey by Rohinton Mistry	$11.00	0-679-73871-1
____ Hopeful Monsters by Nicholas Mosley	$14.00	0-679-73929-7
____ Cities of Salt by Abdelrahman Munif	$16.00	0-394-75526-X
____ The Trench by Abdelrahman Munif	$14.00	0-679-74533-5
____ Variations on Night and Day by Abdelrahman Munif	$12.00	0-679-75551-9
____ Dance Dance Dance by Haruki Murakami	$13.00	0-679-75379-6
____ The Elephant Vanishes by Haruki Murakami	$12.00	0-679-75053-3
____ Hard-Boiled Wonderland and the End of the World by Haruki Murakami	$12.00	0-679-74346-4
____ The Spyglass Tree by Albert Murray	$10.00	0-679-73085-0
____ Ada, or Ardor by Vladimir Nabokov	$16.00	0-679-72522-9
____ Bend Sinister by Vladimir Nabokov	$13.00	0-679-72727-2
____ The Defense by Vladimir Nabokov	$11.00	0-679-72722-1
____ Despair by Vladimir Nabokov	$11.00	0-679-72343-9
____ The Enchanter by Vladimir Nabokov	$10.00	0-679-72886-4
____ The Eye by Vladimir Nabokov	$10.00	0-679-72723-X
____ The Gift by Vladimir Nabokov	$12.00	0-679-72725-6
____ Glory by Vladimir Nabokov	$10.00	0-679-72724-8
____ Invitation to a Beheading by Vladimir Nabokov	$11.00	0-679-72531-8
____ King, Queen, Knave by Vladimir Nabokov	$11.00	0-679-72340-4
____ Laughter in the Dark by Vladimir Nabokov	$12.00	0-679-72450-8

VINTAGE INTERNATIONAL

——— Lolita by Vladimir Nabokov	$10.00	0-679-72316-1
——— Look at the Harlequins! by Vladimir Nabokov	$12.00	0-679-72728-0
——— Mary by Vladimir Nabokov	$10.00	0-679-72620-9
——— Pale Fire by Vladimir Nabokov	$11.00	0-679-72342-0
——— Pnin by Vladimir Nabokov	$10.00	0-679-72341-2
——— The Real Life of Sebastian Knight by Vladimir Nabokov	$11.00	0-679-72726-4
——— Speak, Memory by Vladimir Nabokov	$13.00	0-679-72339-0
——— Strong Opinions by Vladimir Nabokov	$12.00	0-679-72609-8
——— Transparent Things by Vladimir Nabokov	$10.00	0-679-72541-5
——— A Bend in the River by V. S. Naipaul	$10.00	0-679-72202-5
——— Guerrillas by V. S. Naipaul	$12.00	0-679-73174-1
——— A Turn in the South by V. S. Naipaul	$11.00	0-679-72488-5
——— A Way in the World by V. S. Naipaul	$13.00	0-679-76166-7
——— The English Patient by Michael Ondaatje	$11.00	0-679-74520-3
——— Running in the Family by Michael Ondaatje	$10.00	0-679-74669-2
——— Body Snatcher by Juan Carlos Onetti	$13.00	0-679-73887-8
——— Black Box by Amos Oz	$11.00	0-679-72185-1
——— My Michael by Amos Oz	$11.00	0-679-72804-X
——— The Slopes of Lebanon by Amos Oz	$11.00	0-679-73144-X
——— Metaphor and Memory by Cynthia Ozick	$13.00	0-679-73425-2
——— The Shawl by Cynthia Ozick	$7.95	0-679-72926-7
——— Dictionary of the Khazars by Milorad Pavić		
male edition	$13.00	0-679-72461-3
female edition	$13.00	0-679-72754-X
——— Truck Stop Rainbows by Iva Pekárková	$11.00	0-679-74675-7
——— Cambridge by Caryl Phillips	$10.00	0-679-73689-1
——— Crossing the River by Caryl Phillips	$11.00	0-679-75794-5
——— A State of Independence by Caryl Phillips	$10.00	0-679-75930-1
——— The Law of White Spaces by Giorgio Pressburger	$10.00	0-679-75246-3
——— Complete Collected Stories by V. S. Pritchett	$22.00	0-679-73892-4
——— Swann's Way by Marcel Proust	$13.00	0-679-72009-X
——— Kiss of the Spider Woman by Manuel Puig	$11.00	0-679-72449-4
——— Memoirs of an Anti-Semite by Gregor von Rezzori	$12.00	0-679-73182-2
——— The Orient-Express by Gregor von Rezzori	$11.00	0-679-74822-9
——— The Snows of Yesteryear by Gregor von Rezzori	$10.95	0-679-73181-4
——— The Notebooks of Malte Laurids Brigge by Rainer Maria Rilke	$13.00	0-679-73245-4
——— Selected Poetry by Rainer Maria Rilke	$12.00	0-679-72201-7
——— The Breast by Philip Roth	$9.00	0-679-74901-2
——— Goodbye, Columbus by Philip Roth	$11.00	0-679-74826-1
——— The Great American Novel by Philip Roth	$13.00	0-679-74906-3
——— My Life as a Man by Philip Roth	$11.00	0-679-74827-X
——— Operation Shylock by Philip Roth	$12.00	0-679-75029-0
——— Portnoy's Complaint by Philip Roth	$11.00	0-679-75645-0
——— The Professor of Desire by Philip Roth	$10.00	0-679-74900-4
——— When She Was Good by Philip Roth	$12.00	0-679-75925-5
——— Mating by Norman Rush	$12.00	0-679-73709-X
——— Whites by Norman Rush	$10.00	0-679-73816-9
——— Light Years by James Salter	$13.00	0-679-74073-2
——— The Age of Reason by Jean-Paul Sartre	$13.00	0-679-73895-9
——— No Exit and 3 Other Plays by Jean-Paul Sartre	$10.00	0-679-72516-4
——— The Reprieve by Jean-Paul Sartre	$15.00	0-679-74078-3
——— Troubled Sleep by Jean-Paul Sartre	$12.00	0-679-74079-1
——— Open Doors and Three Novellas by Leonardo Sciascia	$12.00	0-679-73561-5
——— Cock and Bull by Will Self	$11.00	0-679-75092-4

VINTAGE INTERNATIONAL

____ **My Idea of Fun** by Will Self	$12.00	0-679-75093-2
____ **All You Who Sleep Tonight** by Vikram Seth	$7.00	0-679-73025-7
____ **The Golden Gate** by Vikram Seth	$13.00	0-679-73457-0
____ **And Quiet Flows the Don** by Mikhail Sholokhov	$15.00	0-679-72521-0
____ **By Grand Central Station I Sat Down and Wept** by Elizabeth Smart	$10.00	0-679-73804-5
____ **In the Eye of the Sun** by Ahdaf Soueif	$15.00	0-679-74932-2
____ **Ake: The Years of Childhood** by Wole Soyinka	$12.00	0-679-72540-7
____ **Isarà: A Voyage Around "Essay"** by Wole Soyinka	$9.95	0-679-73246-2
____ **Children of Light** by Robert Stone	$11.00	0-679-73593-3
____ **A Flag for Sunrise** by Robert Stone	$12.00	0-679-73762-6
____ **Confessions of Nat Turner** by William Styron	$12.00	0-679-73663-8
____ **Lie Down in Darkness** by William Styron	$12.00	0-679-73597-6
____ **The Long March** and **In the Clap Shack** by William Styron	$12.00	0-679-73675-1
____ **Set This House on Fire** by William Styron	$13.00	0-679-73674-3
____ **Sophie's Choice** by William Styron	$13.00	0-679-73637-9
____ **This Quiet Dust** by William Styron	$12.00	0-679-73596-8
____ **A Tidewater Morning** by William Styron	$9.00	0-679-75449-0
____ **Confessions of Zeno** by Italo Svevo	$12.00	0-679-72234-3
____ **Ever After** by Graham Swift	$11.00	0-679-74026-0
____ **Learning to Swim** by Graham Swift	$9.00	0-679-73978-5
____ **Out of This World** by Graham Swift	$10.00	0-679-74032-5
____ **Shuttlecock** by Graham Swift	$10.00	0-679-73933-5
____ **The Sweet-Shop Owner** by Graham Swift	$10.00	0-679-73980-7
____ **Waterland** by Graham Swift	$11.00	0-679-73979-3
____ **The Beautiful Mrs. Seidenman** by Andrzej Szczypiorski	$9.95	0-679-73214-4
____ **Diary of a Mad Old Man** by Junichiro Tanizaki	$10.00	0-679-73024-9
____ **The Key** by Junichiro Tanizaki	$11.00	0-679-73023-0
____ **Quicksand** by Junichiro Tanizaki	$11.00	0-679-76022-9
____ **The Reed Cutter** and **Captain Shigemoto's Mother** by Junichiro Tanizaki	$11.00	0-679-75791-0
____ **On the Golden Porch** by Tatyana Tolstaya	$11.00	0-679-72843-0
____ **Sleepwalker in a Fog** by Tatyana Tolstaya	$11.00	0-679-73063-X
____ **The Real Life of Alejandro Mayta** by Mario Vargas Llosa	$12.00	0-679-72478-8
____ **The Eye of the Story** by Eudora Welty	$11.00	0-679-73004-4
____ **Losing Battles** by Eudora Welty	$12.00	0-679-72882-1
____ **The Optimist's Daughter** by Eudora Welty	$9.00	0-679-72883-X
____ **The Beautiful Room Is Empty** by Edmund White	$11.00	0-679-75540-3
____ **Forgetting Elena** by Edmund White	$10.00	0-679-75573-X
____ **The Passion** by Jeanette Winterson	$10.00	0-679-72437-0
____ **Sexing the Cherry** by Jeanette Winterson	$10.00	0-679-73316-7
____ **Written on the Body** by Jeanette Winterson	$11.00	0-679-74447-9